Will Ka... her c...

Sterling negotiated the next few jumps with boldness and accuracy, and Kaitlin began to relax just a little. Out of the corner of her eye, she could see spectators lining the edge of the course.

Was Connor among them? The unbidden thought came into her mind, temporarily distracting her. Kaitlin's hands closed abruptly on her reins, and Sterling must have felt it—she threw in a little buck of protest at being held back.

"Sorry, girl," Kaitlin mumbled as they tore across the course.

She frowned in concentration when they neared the next fence, which was a tricky upright.

Sterling took it perfectly and afterward tossed her head, begging to be allowed to go faster.

"Save your energy, silly," Kaitlin murmured lovingly to her mare. "We need to finish this course, and that nasty big bank is still up ahead."

She knew she shouldn't think of anything but her next fence, but she found herself trying to scan the crowd, unconsciously slowing Sterling as she did so.

The mare fought against Kaitlin's uncharacteristic hold and galloped on in a zigzag pattern. Suddenly they were in front of the bank.

Bad approach, Kaitlin thought frantically. . . .

Collect all the books in the Thoroughbred series

Collect all the books in the Ashleigh series

*coming soon

THOROUGHBRED

KAITLIN'S WILD RIDE

CREATED BY

JOANNA CAMPBELL

WRITTEN BY

KARLE DICKERSON

HarperEntertainment
An Imprint of HarperCollinsPublishers

HarperEntertainment
An Imprint of HarperCollins*Publishers*
10 East 53rd Street, New York, NY 10022-5299

Produced by 17th Street Productions,
an Alloy Online, Inc., company

ISBN 0-06-073813-8

First printing: November 2004

Printed in the United States of America

Visit HarperEntertainment on the World Wide Web at
www.harpercollins.com

❖ 10 9 8 7 6 5 4 3 2 1

To Earl Gray, Cezanne, Mr. Knightley, Molly, and Magpie, some of the finest horses and ponies ever to have set hooves in a paddock

KAITLIN'S WILD RIDE

1

"AAGH! I CAN'T PULL OFF MY BOOTS, AND MY MOM WILL BE HERE any minute!" wailed little Penny Saunders, barging into Whisperwood's tack room, her pigtails flying. "Kaitlin, have you seen my bootjack?"

Seventeen-year-old Kaitlin Boyce looked up from the breastplate she was saddle-soaping as her student ran into the room.

"Whoa, there." Kaitlin smiled at Penny. "Crank down the volume. Your bootjack's right where you left it this morning—under your dirty saddle pad. And, ahem, notice that I used the word *dirty*."

"Thanks!" the little girl exclaimed, whirling around. "I'll wash it, I promise." She dashed out the door, but turned around just as she reached the threshold. "Um, Kaitlin? Where is it, exactly?"

"Under the protective vest that some *other* forgetful student left behind this morning," replied Kaitlin with a small smile. She wiped the breastplate with a soft cloth. "The last I saw it, it was—"

"Sam said you could tell me where Bouncer's breastplate is!" Justin yelled, piling into the tack room behind Penny. "I'm late for my lesson, and I *reeeally* need it!"

Just then yet another student ran into the room alongside Christina Reese and Allie Avery.

"Where are Jelly Roll's galloping boots?" the student asked Christina, tugging at her sleeve.

"Maybe Kaitlin knows," replied Christina, who, while recuperating from her recent track accident, was teaching beginners at Whisperwood along with fourteen-year-old Allie.

Allie chimed in, "Yeah, Kaitlin knows where *everything* is."

At the sound of Allie's voice, Kaitlin stiffened. She liked Allie well enough and had made a point to be nice to her when she'd moved to nearby Tall Oaks after her father died. But ever since the fourteen-year-old girl had started helping out at Whisperwood, Kaitlin felt strangely competitive with her. It didn't help that Allie always seemed to worm her way onto Kaitlin's horse whenever Kaitlin couldn't ride. Kaitlin knew that Allie had also ridden Christina's racehorse, Star, and she wondered how Christina could stand for Allie to ride him when she couldn't.

The sound of a blaring car horn interrupted Kaitlin's thoughts.

"I'm coming, Mom!" shouted Penny at the top of her lungs. Turning toward Kaitlin, she added, "I keep telling her Sam says not to honk like that!"

Penny was referring to Samantha Nelson, who owned Whisperwood with her husband, Tor.

"C'mon, Kaitlin. Tell me where the breastplate is!" Justin demanded.

Just then the muffled ringing sound of the portable phone came from somewhere in the tack room. Kaitlin began rummaging around looking for the source of the ringing, while Justin stamped his foot.

"Hurry," Justin said anxiously. "Christina and Allie are waiting!"

"One second." Kaitlin held up a finger as she finally located the phone under a pile of tack Sam had set aside to be donated to the Thoroughbred Retirement Foundation. Frowning at Justin, she spoke into the receiver.

"Hello, Mrs. Townsend . . . No, Parker's not here. I think he's out on the cross-country course with Tor," she said with forced patience, holding the phone away from her ear. "Yes, ma'am . . . Right away, ma'am. I'll tell him that you're trying to reach him and that he'd better turn on his cell phone."

Kaitlin hung up and brushed back her sun-streaked brown hair. "What a witch! Like Parker's supposed to take her call while he's leaping four-foot oxers at warp speed!" she muttered. Then she turned toward Penny and Justin. "Okay, you two, first things first. You both have to chill. You know there's no shouting in the barn. You'll scare the horses."

Penny dropped her head. "Sorry," she mumbled.

"But I need the breastplate," insisted Justin.

"Bootjack—on the bench in Sam's office. Breastplate—right here. Freshly saddle-soaped," Kaitlin rapped out, and handed Justin the gleaming piece of equipment.

"Thanks!" Justin and Penny chorused as they raced away.

Kaitlin watched the two students depart and shook her head before turning back to putting away the soap and dirty rags. Sometimes it was hard being the organized type, especially at a sport-horse training barn as busy as Whisperwood.

Where's this? Where's that? Ask Kaitlin. Kaitlin will know.

But, Kaitlin thought with a grin, being organized had its positive points as well. She knew that many of the great opportunities she'd gotten were because she made it her business to keep track of details. Sam had recently announced that she was pregnant with twins, and now she was asking Kaitlin to help out around the barn, and even with the beginning riders.

On occasion Kaitlin had been asked to groom for several of Sam's top eventing clients at major events, too. One of those clients included Kaitlin's hero and instructor, Parker Townsend. Just this past April, Kaitlin had groomed for him at Rolex, one of eventing's most prestigious horse trials.

Kaitlin had been thrilled to play a role, however small, in the exciting competition. Though she'd been disappointed when Parker had pulled his beloved horse Foxglove at the last minute, she'd definitely understood. Plus, Parker's concern had paid off, and the mare had been in top form for her next big challenge: Burghley, a big four-star event held in England. Parker and Foxy had done well at Burghley, coming in fourth.

Kaitlin had recently taken Sterling Dream, the horse she leased from Sam, to a preliminary event, so she had a feel for just how difficult an event such as Burghley was. She couldn't wait for the day when she, too, rode in international competitions. The only thing that seemed to matter to her these days was improving her dressage and jumping so that one day she could compete with other world-class riders.

Of course, I've got to get over my leaning problem first,

Kaitlin thought, making a face. Since starting her senior year at Henry Clay High School, she'd had to cancel a maddening number of lessons due to various senior activities. Before she knew it, she'd fallen back into the old bad habit she'd thought she'd licked. Because she was right-handed, her right leg tended to be stronger and sink heavily into her right stirrup. This caused her to lean, which hurt her performance both on the flat and over the bigger jumps. She was trying her hardest to correct her seat, but missing lessons hadn't helped any. And since she was scheduled to compete in a local two-day horse trial in just two weeks, she was really starting to worry.

"I'll be lucky if I even get around the cross-country course at Deep Woods at all, the way I'm going," Kaitlin muttered dismally. She resisted the impulse to gnaw on her already bitten-down fingernails.

But then she brightened, thinking about Sterling, the gorgeous dapple-gray Thoroughbred she'd been lucky enough to ride. As far as she was concerned, Sterling was the best horse in the world. It had been a magical day when Sam bought the talented eventer from Christina so that Christina could devote herself to preparing Star for a racing career. Sam had leased Sterling to Kaitlin, and immediately Kaitlin knew that she and the mare would make great partners.

Kaitlin glanced at her watch and noticed that it was

four-thirty—nearly time for her lesson. She had already groomed Sterling, so all that remained was to put on the mare's wraps and saddle her up. Donning her helmet and gloves, Kaitlin hurried over to Sterling's stall. The gray mare nickered when she saw Kaitlin coming down the aisle, though she'd seen her only an hour before, when Kaitlin had arrived after school.

"Hey, girl," Kaitlin called lovingly as she opened the stall door. She reached up and stroked Sterling's glossy, black-tipped ears. Then she planted a kiss on her soft muzzle. After running her hands through her silky mane, Kaitlin put on the mare's leather halter and led her to the cross ties. Then she double-checked Sterling's feet, put on her polo wraps, and tacked her up.

A few minutes later, Kaitlin mounted, rode out to the outdoor arena, and began her warm-up. As Sterling's muscles loosened, she stretched out her lovely, long neck, and her strides lengthened. Kaitlin pushed her heels down and sucked in the cool Kentucky air. Now that it was early November, the trees were dropping leaves, and Kaitlin smiled appreciatively at how the golden sunlight played against the last of the fall foliage.

Christina and Allie's students were in the indoor arena, and Kaitlin and Sterling had the outdoor ring to themselves.

Good thing, Kaitlin thought. The last thing she needed

was an audience of little kids observing her riding mistakes.

Soon Kaitlin urged Sterling into a working trot. She and the mare had just completed three circuits when Parker appeared on the rise. From the distance, Kaitlin could see Foxy's mahogany bay coat glinting in the sun, her powerful muscles rippling.

"I'll be right there," Parker called, riding toward her. "Just want to finish cooling Foxy."

Kaitlin held up her crop to acknowledge Parker before turning back to her warm-up.

She hadn't been able to have that many lessons with Parker lately. He'd been gone all summer in England, and since coming back, he was busier than ever spending time with his girlfriend, Christina, while she recuperated from her injuries and schooling his three eventers, Foxy, Ozzie, and Black Hawke. On top of that, he was attending clinics and flying back and forth to meet with Captain Donnelly, the chef d'equipe for the United States Equestrian Team.

Parker won't be happy when he sees that I've backslid so much lately, Kaitlin thought.

A few minutes later Parker entered the ring, still mounted on Foxy. He was wearing his University of Kentucky sweatshirt, now drenched with perspiration and covered with mud. He rode on the buckle, so that Foxy could relax after her workout over Whisperwood's demanding cross-country course.

"How was Foxy?" Kaitlin asked as she continued posting around the ring. She always enjoyed hearing about other people's rides. She had gotten some of her best tips by listening to top eventers such as Parker describe their strategies.

Parker grinned, taking off his helmet and shaking his wet hair. "Perfecto, as usual," he said happily. "I totally focused on accuracy today, and it paid off. Foxy was unbelievable—especially over the toadstools."

"Cool," Kaitlin replied, wishing she were as confident as Parker always seemed to be. "Oh, by the way, your mom called."

A shadow crossed Parker's handsome, angular face. "What a surprise," he said sarcastically. "She probably wants me to race home and climb into my dinner jacket for another one of her boring, glitzy galas."

Kaitlin made sympathetic noises. She hated how Parker's parents always treated him as though he should just drop everything—especially Foxy—whenever they barked out orders. "She didn't mention any boring gala, but she wants you to turn on your cell and call her back," she remarked. "She was awfully, um, *adamant.*"

Parker ignored her comment and instead focused in on Kaitlin's leg.

"There you go again, sinking more weight into your right heel," he barked in a businesslike tone.

"Maybe you ought to call her before we start," Kaitlin said, shifting in her saddle. She knew Parker would probably forget, and she didn't want Lavinia Townsend to think she hadn't passed on the message.

"Maybe you ought to concentrate on balancing your weight instead of worrying about mother dearest," he replied. "We don't have that much time till it gets dark, and you and I have a lot of work to do."

Kaitlin knew better than to push it. Parker could be pretty stubborn.

"Now, let's see," Parker said, riding into the center of the ring and stopping to observe her. "I want you to go around at an even pace without falling over, like you're doing now."

Kaitlin scowled. "Bleagh," she muttered. "Welcome to the Leaning Zone."

"Have you been doing your exercises to help strengthen your left leg?" Parker asked.

Making a face, Kaitlin adjusted her weight. "Not as much as I should," she admitted. "Man, I thought I had this problem solved once and for all. But now look at me. What a nightmare."

"Believe me, I know how discouraging it is when old bad habits resurface," Parker said. "But you've gotta keep at it, otherwise you'll throw Sterling off over the big sticks, and your dressage scores will suffer. I've said it a zillion times, but eventing's all about balance."

"I know, I know." Kaitlin jammed her helmet down more firmly on her head and continued around the arena. "I'm working on it."

"Relax," Parker called as he studied her. "We're going to work on transitions. Now that you're riding preliminary, you're going to be seeing lots of 'em in your dressage tests."

"Mmm," Kaitlin mumbled, trying to concentrate.

Parker watched intently for a few moments. "You're grinding your teeth," he said. "And you're starting to muscle it. All the way from where I'm sitting, I can feel your tension. So can Sterling. That's why she's wringing her tail."

Kaitlin took a deep breath and tried to position herself correctly. It was easy as long as she was going down the straightaway. As soon as she entered the turn, however, it was a different story. She could feel her right seat bone dig deeper into her saddle than her left. She didn't need to turn around to know that Sterling's tail was still wringing. Kaitlin felt herself drift slightly off center, and she adjusted her seat again. She came out of the turn and trotted down the straightaway.

"Better," Parker called out. "See if you can stay centered while you make a twenty-meter circle."

After Kaitlin circled, Parker asked her to return to the rail.

"That wasn't bad. But I'll say it again: You've got to

11

lighten up. Now let's see some transitions," Parker said. "And don't overbend to the inside. Flex Sterling a little to the outside."

Kaitlin winced as she started flexing and felt herself tilt slightly. She cued Sterling into a downward transition while she tried to right herself. Sterling responded by returning to the walk, but because she was unbalanced, she fell to the inside heavily.

My fault, thought Kaitlin. She adjusted her seat and, without collecting Sterling, asked for an upward transition. Sterling walked a few extra steps before moving into the trot.

"Get organized before asking for a transition," Parker hollered.

Though Kaitlin tried to gather her mare squarely under her, she knew that she wasn't balanced at all. As a result, Sterling stumbled slightly a few seconds later when Kaitlin asked for the downward transition back to the walk. Pulling up, Kaitlin took off her helmet for a few seconds and blew out an impatient breath.

"That wasn't right," she muttered.

"Try again," Parker said patiently. "Transitions are key."

The next attempts were no better. Kaitlin could feel her face reddening.

"You're still tensing up," Parker told her. "Sterling wants to give you her best, but you're sending her all kinds of mixed signals."

"Sorry," Kaitlin murmured to her horse as she gave Parker a little wave. "I'll try harder."

For the next half hour, Kaitlin battled on, struggling to ride with a relaxed seat and keep her weight even. By the time her lesson was over, she was perspiring from her effort. Sterling's sweat-soaked neck was a dark pewter color.

"Let's quit on this for now," Parker said. "I think Sterling's had enough."

"I'm sorry, girl," Kaitlin murmured, patting her mare. "I'm riding terribly, and you just keep doing your job like you're supposed to."

She was horrified to feel a frustrated tear slip down her cheek.

"Aw, ease up, Triple Threat," Parker said, looking worried. Parker had coined her nickname about a month ago when he saw that her confidence was starting to slip big time. He'd told her it meant that she had brains, determination, and talent—and that she'd better not ever forget it. "You'll sort it out before you know it."

Kaitlin scrubbed hastily at her eyes and sighed. "I hope that's before my next trial."

"You will," Parker replied.

"Maybe I'll stay here and ride a bit more till I get it right," Kaitlin said forcefully.

Parker shook his head. "Nope. Give it a rest and call it a day. It's Friday, after all."

"Sam will leave the arena lights on for me if I want—even if it *is* Friday," Kaitlin pointed out.

"True," Parker said. "But you really ought to forget about riding. It wouldn't hurt to just clear your head and go kick up your heels someplace where there aren't any horses. You know, go see Henry Clay High whomp Lexington High at football or something."

Kaitlin wrinkled her nose. "Gross. You know I don't go to football games." She snorted.

Parker grinned. "Just testing ya," he said. "But seriously, go do something fun tonight instead."

Kaitlin was puzzled. "Something fun? Well, I did just get this new DVD I've been dying to watch, called *Eventing Greats.*"

Parker raised an eyebrow. *"Eventing Greats?"*

Kaitlin nodded and babbled on eagerly. "It's got highlights of all the biggies—Burghley, Badminton, Rolex, the British Open Eventing Championships, and a whole bunch of others. I think I'll just curl up at home and watch the whole thing—if I can keep my little sisters from bugging me. I can freeze the frames and really study the positions of the top riders in the game. Cool, huh?"

Parker gazed at her with his smoky gray eyes. "Ambition is great and all, but there is such a thing as turning into a grind, you know. You ought to be a kid while you still can and go have a good time with some of your high school friends."

"You sound like the Wise Old Man on the Mountain instead of a college student," Kaitlin teased.

"Gee, thanks," Parker replied. "But it still doesn't change what I'm saying."

"Whatever, Parker," Kaitlin flared. "I don't really have high school friends anymore. Can I help it that my buds were mostly seniors last year and that they graduated in June? Your girlfriend among them. And Melanie. There just aren't a lot of people to hang with now at school."

"Sure there are. How about, oh, say, Alicia Lathrop?" Parker asked. "I've always wondered why you two weren't better friends. I mean, you take lessons together sometimes and all. And she's a senior, right?"

"Guys are so blind," Kaitlin said. "In case you haven't noticed, she's changed a lot in the last few months. Look how many lessons she's canceled lately."

"So have you, from what I've heard," Parker replied quietly.

"That's different," Kaitlin shot back. "I've had all these community service commitments at school that I've put off, and I can't get out of them. Alicia cancels her lessons because she's gone completely boy-crazy. She only rides these days because she gets sports credit at school and needs her credits to graduate next June."

"Well, anyway, last I checked, there were twelve hundred students at Henry Clay High," Parker countered. "So doesn't that make, like, three hundred in the senior class?

15

Surely there are a few worth getting to know."

"Maybe," Kaitlin replied impatiently. "But none of them are horse people. None of them event."

"News flash: There's more to life than eventing," Parker said evenly.

Kaitlin burst into laughter. "You're one to talk, Mr. USET-obsessed," she commented. "Aren't you going to some lecture at eight o'clock at the Horse Park on conditioning your eventer? Talk about a wild Friday night!"

Parker winked. "Do as I say, not as I do," he said, grinning. With that, he turned Foxy toward the arena gate and headed toward the barn.

2

"Go make friends. Go to football games," Kaitlin muttered with disgust as she watched Parker ride off. She shook her head and loosened Sterling's girth a notch. She lengthened her reins so that her mare could drop her neck and relax, but at the same time Kaitlin felt her own shoulders tightening up. By the time the mare was completely cooled, Kaitlin's whole body ached. Her leg cramped when she lifted it over her saddle, and she grimaced when she hit the ground. Her boots had gotten soaked the previous weekend when she'd gone to a nearby jumper show with Tor and ridden in a few jumper classes to prepare for Deep Woods. In her last class, she'd sailed over a fence and had fallen into the liverpool. The leather shrank when it dried, so now her boots constricted her feet.

I'm a mess, and it's my own stupid fault for riding so badly, Kaitlin thought, loosening Sterling's girth even more and running up her stirrup irons. She took off her helmet and slicked a wet strand of hair behind her ear. No doubt about it, she decided. She needed to get a grip on her riding problem, and quickly.

I'll soak in the tub tonight, she thought, leading Sterling back to the barn. *Then I'll watch the DVD, and maybe, just maybe, I'll figure out a way to push past my leaning problem. At least I hope so.*

For a split second, she pictured herself plummeting down the hill after the big bank at Deep Woods....

"Why the long face?" a voice said, breaking Kaitlin's reverie.

Kaitlin snapped her head up. She'd been so immersed in her thoughts, she hadn't seen Sam coming down the barn aisle toward her.

"Uh, um, hi," she stammered. She glanced involuntarily at Sam's thickening waist and marveled at how slim Sam still looked, even though she was carrying twins.

Sam brushed back her auburn hair and tilted her head. "You didn't answer my question," she said.

Kaitlin sighed. "Oh, I just had another crummy lesson," she muttered. "Guess I'm on a losing roll. Maybe I ought to take up knitting or something instead of riding."

Sam shuddered in mock horror. "No need to go to that

extreme. You just need some consistency to attack a few riding issues. And remember, good riders always need to work on something."

"Some more than others," grumbled Kaitlin, hating how often people reminded her of her missed lessons.

"*All* riders have their ups and downs," Sam said firmly. "That's part of the game."

"Why does it have to be so hard?" Kaitlin suddenly heard herself wail.

Omigosh, I sound just like a whiny little kid in a lead line class, she thought, startled at the tone in her voice.

"Riding's supposed to be hard," Sam replied. "If it were so easy, it wouldn't be worth trying to do."

Kaitlin grinned weakly and nodded.

"Now go home, forget about riding for a bit, and have some fun," Sam said, walking on.

Everyone's always telling me to go have fun, Kaitlin thought darkly as she led Sterling to the cross ties and pulled off her saddle and bridle. She placed the saddle on a nearby portable rack and hung her bridle on the hook. Grabbing a damp sponge, she wiped off Sterling's bit.

"Ow! That's my foot you're stepping on, horse breath!" shrieked Madison Henley in the next cross tie. The tall blonde was grooming Snicker, one of the new school horses Tor had just bought at auction. Madison had moved to Lexington over the summer and started school at Henry Clay

19

in the fall. Recently she'd started taking lessons at Whisper-wood, but Kaitlin didn't know her very well, since Madison rode with a lower-level group. In the barn aisles, Kaitlin had been too shy to try to talk to the self-assured girl.

"You okay? Need help?" she called out automatically.

Madison shook her head. "No, thanks—crisis over," she muttered. "It was just a quick stomp-and-run."

Kaitlin picked up her grooming tote and pulled out a soft brush. "Good thing they make riding boots with metal toes," she said conversationally. *Maybe*, she thought, *I ought to do what Parker said and try to make some new friends—starting with this girl.*

Madison studied her for a few seconds. "I know I've seen you somewhere besides this barn. You're a senior, like me, right? Henry Clay High?"

"Yeah. I'm Kaitlin Boyce, by the way," Kaitlin replied, taking off her gloves. "You're in the homecoming court, right?"

Madison laughed and turned back to her horse. "Guess I'm kind of hard to miss."

Kaitlin considered that remark for a second as she started grooming Sterling. It had sounded as if Madison was bragging. But soon she forgot about Madison and began mentally reriding her lesson. If only she could figure out a surefire way to maintain a balanced seat! There had to be a way if she just put her mind to it. She was sure she and

20

Sterling would be unbeatable, not only at the next horse trial, but at the more competitive ones as well.

"Hel-*lo*! I was talking to you," she suddenly heard Madison say impatiently.

"Sorry," Kaitlin mumbled, turning to the girl and trying to focus. "I was thinking about something—my lesson, actually."

"Don't even talk to me about lessons!" Madison replied.

"Why not?" asked Kaitlin, her ears perking up. "Did you have a bad one, too?" She waited eagerly for her answer. Maybe, she thought, she and Madison could exchange ideas for solutions.

Madison picked up her horse's foot. "It was all right," she said, hacking away at Snicker's frog with a hoof pick in a way that made Kaitlin wince. Madison looked around and lowered her voice. "Actually, though, I don't know why I ride at all. I think it's completely boring. But my mom says I'd better have a decent extracurricular activity for when I apply to college. I chose riding because it'll impress the admissions people."

Kaitlin blinked. She couldn't imagine riding just to try to look good on some college application.

"Oh," she said weakly.

Madison didn't seem to notice Kaitlin's reaction. "Riding's bad enough. But I wish I could pay a groom to do this

21

disgusting stuff," she muttered, wrinkling her nose while she continued picking out Snicker's hooves. "At the riding school I was at in Chicago, we just climbed off after lessons and that was that."

Kaitlin turned back to Sterling, not sure what to say. As far as she was concerned, caring for horses was just as much fun as riding.

"Of course, Whisperwood has one *suh-weet* attraction," Madison went on. "Parker Townsend. Now *there's* a reason to show up for lessons, if you know what I mean."

Kaitlin tried not to let her annoyance show. The idea of anyone scoping her hero made her crazy. "He won't be around long. He's one of the USET's developing riders, and he has to leave at the end of January to train," she said. She couldn't help being proud when she said it. She was keenly aware that Parker was crushed that he hadn't been chosen for the team, but Kaitlin knew that being a developing rider was still a big deal.

Madison looked at her blankly. Obviously she had no idea what Kaitlin was talking about. "*Developing* rider?" Madison exclaimed. "I thought Parker already *was* a rider."

Developing rider as in the Olympics, featherbrain, Kaitlin wanted to say. But she knew a girl like Madison would understand only one thing: that he was already taken. Aloud she said, "He's got a girlfriend, you know."

"Duh. Everyone knows that. Christina Reese, big-time

jockey wonder girl, now on crutches," Madison replied. "But girlfriends aren't always forever. I heard that they broke up for a while. They could break up again."

"Don't bet on it," Kaitlin said under her breath, licking her finger and wiping a spot off Sterling's coat.

Madison shrugged. "Oh, who cares? Quite honestly, Parker's a little too horse-crazy for me. Know what I mean?" She gazed expressionlessly at Kaitlin, who was patting Sterling lovingly. "No, maybe you don't."

Kaitlin went back to brushing Sterling without comment.

Well, cross Madison Henley off the potential-friend list, she thought grumpily.

The next day she'd take Sterling on a fitness gallop. That cheered Kaitlin up and made her put annoying girls such as Madison out of her mind.

That evening after dinner, Kaitlin went into the living room carrying her DVD. To her dismay, she saw that her little sisters were already firmly planted in front of the screen watching a movie they'd seen at least a hundred times.

"Hey, guys, want to see some really great horses jumping big fences?" Kaitlin said, sounding like a salesperson.

"Not a chance," said Jordan, her eyes never leaving the screen.

"You can watch yours when we're done," chirped Lindy.

"Fine," said Kaitlin, too tired to argue.

She went to her room with the intention of heading back down later to watch her eventing tape, but within minutes of climbing into her bed with a copy of the USCTA *Omnibus*, she'd fallen sound asleep.

"All right, girl. You ready to rip?" Kaitlin asked Sterling as she hooked her into the cross ties the next morning. Sterling pawed the ground and snorted impatiently.

"She definitely looks like she's firing up her engines," said Tor, who was leading Crescendo, a client's gelding, down the aisle. "The farrier shod her this morning, so she's good to go. Want some company? Crescendo and I will join you if you'd like. This pretty boy needs to stretch his legs."

Kaitlin grinned and nodded. "That'd be great. Sterling likes it better when she's got someone to race against," she replied. "Reminds her of her days on the track, I guess."

Tor grinned. "I'll be out in the field waiting for you."

After Kaitlin saddled Sterling, she put on her brightly colored helmet and led the mare from the barn. She could see Tor trotting Crescendo just behind the main arena. At the sight of her friend, Sterling tossed her lovely head and began toe-dancing.

"Save your energy, Sterling," Kaitlin said, laughing.

She climbed up into the saddle and placed her feet in the irons. Sterling lurched forward, straining to join Crescendo in the field. Kaitlin closed her gloved fingers on the reins. "Not yet," she murmured to her mare.

"Sterling's going to be hard to hold today," Tor observed when Kaitlin and Sterling approached.

"A little, maybe," Kaitlin admitted. "She's full of herself, but she always comes back to me when I ask."

"Well, you've done a good job schooling her, that's for sure," Tor said as they began their warm-up trot. "From what I've been hearing, you two are going to give the competition a run for their money at Deep Woods in two weeks."

Kaitlin looked ahead between Sterling's ears. Clearly Tor hadn't gotten the word about how badly she'd been riding lately. "How'd you miss out on the news?" Kaitlin muttered in a low voice.

Tor glanced at her. "What news?"

"Nothing," Kaitlin said, looking at her stopwatch. "Wasn't important." She shook her head, trying to clear her mind. She didn't want anything to mess with the moment, not when she had a fitness gallop to look forward to. "You ready? We're about to give you and Crescendo a run for your money right now," she bragged.

Tor laughed as he shortened his stirrups. "Confident, aren't we? You sound just like Parker."

"I do?" Kaitlin grinned from ear to ear and turned Sterling toward the three-thousand-meter track that was marked around the field. "I can't think of a better compliment."

With that, she yelled, "Go!" and squeezed Sterling's sides gently. They started up the hill, Crescendo and Tor only slightly behind them.

The sun was just peeking over the trees, and the hills were bathed in soft morning light. Sterling strained against the bit, wanting to flash early speed, but Kaitlin held her to an easy loping canter. She knew better than to expend all Sterling's energy early on. It was far better to pace the mare and spread out her energy during her gallops. Kaitlin sat lightly in her saddle, her body moving rhythmically with the gentle, rocking motion.

She closed her eyes for a few seconds, lost in the sensation of being one with her horse. When she heard Crescendo's hooves pounding beside her, she opened her eyes again. She was glad to see that Crescendo wasn't blowing very hard yet. Just a few months before, the gelding couldn't have gone this long without becoming winded. Lately, however, Tor had been conditioning the gelding for his owner, and now he showed little signs of tiring.

But here comes the test, Kaitlin thought. She took another look at her stopwatch and signaled to Tor that she was about to gallop. Could Crescendo continue to keep up with Sterling?

Kaitlin closed her calves against Sterling's sides, urging the mare into a gallop. She'd gallop her a thousand meters, then check her pulse and respiration. This would help her determine how Sterling was dealing with the pace.

After a while Kaitlin glanced over her shoulder and saw that Crescendo had fallen behind. But she and Sterling galloped on. She lengthened the mare's stride and felt her own blood pumping as the two of them whipped along the track. Every so often she felt herself sinking into her right stirrup, so she tried to correct herself immediately. But soon she was right back where she'd started, off balance and tilting to one side.

"I'm hopeless!" Kaitlin muttered, adjusting her seat for what seemed like the thousandth time.

She and Sterling had almost finished their gallop when suddenly Kaitlin felt the mare take a misstep.

That's because I was leaning again! The thought instantly crossed Kaitlin's mind. The misstep was slight, almost imperceptible, yet Kaitlin brought Sterling down to a walk right away. She looked around to see if Tor was anywhere near to help, but he was already a ways off, walking Crescendo across the field.

Briefly, Kaitlin considered what she ought to do first. It was like triage in a hospital emergency room, prioritizing immediate needs. *Respiration,* she decided quickly. *Then legs.*

Leaping out of the saddle, Kaitlin pulled out her equine stethoscope from her pocket. She pressed the instrument to Sterling's chest, all the while walking the mare in a little circle. Satisfied with the reading, she slipped the stethoscope back into her pocket.

Kaitlin ran her hands down Sterling's legs. When she got to Sterling's left foreleg, she thought she detected a little heat. It was so slight she wasn't sure if it was her imagination. But when she led the mare forward, she saw her head bob.

Something's definitely wrong, Kaitlin thought, her heart leaping to her throat. She loosened Sterling's girth and ran up her stirrup irons while she cooled Sterling and slowly led her back to the barn. By the time they arrived at the barn door, she saw that Sterling was favoring her left leg slightly.

"What happened?" Sam asked, her brow furrowing as she studied Sterling coming toward her.

"I'm not sure," Kaitlin replied. "We were galloping along perfectly, and suddenly she just stepped wrong. I got off right away, but she's not moving the way she should."

Kaitlin didn't say what was nagging at the back of her mind—that she was afraid it might be her fault.

3

"Hmmm. I don't feel any heat," Sam said after running her expert fingers up and down Sterling's left leg. "Still, something's not quite right. I can have Dr. Tanner look at her. He's over in the other barn checking on Curious. Start hosepiping that leg to keep down any inflammation."

Fighting back tears, Kaitlin slowly led Sterling to the wash racks, where she began applying cold water to her leg. It wasn't bad enough that her lessons had been so disastrous lately. Now this.

What if it's something really bad? Kaitlin thought, swallowing hard. Her shoulders slumped as she watched the water rushing onto Sterling's leg. That was the thing about horses. They could go along just fine for months when

29

suddenly—whammo!—one little thing, and they were dead lame. A rider could hope, plan, and work, only to see all her dreams go up in smoke in a few seconds.

It seemed like forever until Sam appeared at the wash racks with Dr. Tanner.

"Heard you needed my attention," the vet said to Kaitlin, setting down his medical bag. He stroked the mare's neck and allowed her to snuffle his palm.

Kaitlin nodded unhappily and explained what had happened.

She bit her lip as Dr. Tanner began his examination. When he was finished, he patted Sterling's shoulder.

"Your mare is a little tender, but I just don't see anything," he said to Kaitlin. Turning to Sam, he added, "Of course, we could do an ultrasound if this persists. Let's see how it goes and rest her for a couple of days. I really think you'll be able to bring her back to full work by the end of the week."

"The end of the week," Kaitlin echoed. She realized how lucky she was that it wasn't worse. But she couldn't help thinking that even if everything was okay, she and Sterling would now lose several precious days of work, with the horse trial only two weeks away.

"That's certainly good news," Sam said to the vet, and flashed a smile to Kaitlin.

Kaitlin sagged against Sterling's shoulder after Sam and

the vet had walked on to check some of the broodmares, and she let out a deep sigh. It was amazing how joyful she'd felt galloping along one minute and how devastated she felt the next.

Guess I'd better focus on the positive, she thought glumly.

Slowly Kaitlin walked Sterling back to her stall, feeling her frustration mounting in spite of her determination to look on the bright side. The next few days were going to drag on forever if she couldn't ride Sterling! And when she started riding again, she knew, it would take time before she and Sterling were back up to form. She'd be a mess at the Deep Woods trial. Every time she started to feel as though she was getting closer to her dream, something happened to set her back.

Well, maybe Sam will let me ride Scooter or one of Tor's jumpers, Kaitlin thought, trying to cheer herself up. By riding other horses, she could at least maintain her muscle tone while Sterling recuperated.

After taking off Sterling's halter, Kaitlin stood quietly beside her in the deep straw, stroking her glossy coat while Sterling bumped her with her soft, velvety muzzle. It was clear that the sensitive mare was trying to make her feel better. That only made Kaitlin feel guiltier, which made everything seem ten times worse.

I'd better go home and stop hanging around here feeling sorry for myself, Kaitlin thought after a while.

31

Just then Sterling lifted her head at the sound of a horse being led into the stall on the other side of the wall.

"Ouch. Stupid horse stepped on me. That's twice in two days." Madison's irritated voice shot through the stall wall.

Maybe you ought to watch where you put your foot, Kaitlin thought, feeling mean. But she couldn't help it. Anyone who rode horses just to try to get into some snooty college had it coming.

"Hey, Madison, are you going to Michaela Parsons's party tonight?" Kaitlin heard Alicia Lathrop say.

Michaela Parsons's sweet sixteen party, Kaitlin thought. She remembered that her mom had recently mentioned the big society bash Michaela's parents were having for their daughter. Her parents were friends with Michaela's parents, since they lived down the street and ran into each other often. Privately Kaitlin thought the Parsons family was really shallow and showy. Michaela was nice enough, but she and Kaitlin had nothing in common. Mrs. Boyce had been thrilled that Kaitlin had been invited, and she hadn't been too happy when Kaitlin told her that she wasn't going.

"I dunno," said Madison. "Is it worth it? I mean, I've been to a zillion sweet sixteens, and they're starting to bore me."

"Well, this one ought to be fun. Michaela's got this humongous house with a guest house filled with video games and foosball and stuff. There's a big terrace by the pool where everyone can dance," Kaitlin heard Alicia say. "It's being catered, and her cousin's band will be playing. They're really good. She promised him a big crowd, so she told me to let everyone know about it."

"Maybe I'll come, then," Madison said. "Who else will be there?"

"Oh, lots of people. Her parents are hoping for a crowd so that maybe the newspaper will cover it in the society pages. Michaela and I put the word out around at school. And I told a couple of kids here at the barn. Body stuffing, you know," Alicia replied. "In fact, I'm looking for Kaitlin so I can tell her. You seen her? Is she still around?"

Kaitlin heard Madison laugh. "You mean Kaitlin Boyce? Are you kidding? Don't bother. She'll never go. She's one of *those*—doesn't think about anything but horses."

"Yeah, true. Very true," came Alicia's voice.

Kaitlin froze as she listened to the two girls giggle. She wasn't sure which made her angrier, being considered only as body stuffing or being accused of thinking only about horses, as if it were something bad!

I do so think about other things besides horses, she thought angrily. But then she let out a huffy breath. She had to admit that maybe Madison wasn't too far off. She hadn't thought of much else lately. And for what? It sure hadn't improved her riding. And now she'd managed to hurt Sterling as well!

"I just can't get anything right, can I?" Kaitlin whispered to her mare while she put on her thick blanket. Stepping out of the stall, she closed the door. While she walked down the barn aisle, she winced. Her body ached all over with tension, and her boots were killing her.

Kaitlin stepped inside the tack room, sat down on the worn wooden bench, and took off her boots, wiggling her cramped toes and nibbling on her thumbnail. She gazed around the tack room, watching dust motes dancing in the sunlight pouring through the windows. Kaitlin scowled as the happy laughter of students returning from lessons drifted down the barn aisle.

Just then Alicia came into the tack room, carrying one of the riding school's saddles. Kaitlin studied her for a few seconds, noting her brightly painted nails and tiny T-shirt that exposed her stomach. She definitely didn't look like most of the serious students around Whisperwood, but Kaitlin had to admit that she appeared happy—and carefree. And that was what struck Kaitlin the most.

Kaitlin glanced down at her own bitten nails and wet, horsehair-covered T-shirt.

"Hey," Alicia said absently, giving Kaitlin a brief nod. She carelessly tossed the saddle over a rack so that it teetered precariously.

Without thinking, Kaitlin leaped up to catch the saddle and saw that Alicia was giving her a weird look.

"You should loosen up a little, you know?" Alicia said, almost pityingly.

"Yeah," Kaitlin mumbled, feeling a little embarrassed. "I just thought it was going to fall."

Alicia turned without replying and headed toward the door.

"About Michaela's party . . ." The words came out of Kaitlin's mouth before she even realized it.

Alicia stopped and looked over her shoulder. "What about it?"

"I, um, overheard you and Madison mention it," Kaitlin plunged on. "I was thinking about going. See you there."

"Uh, yeah," Alicia said, raising her eyebrows. "See you there."

Okay, Boyce, now you've done it. Why did you tell Alicia you'd go to the party? Kaitlin thought later, sitting in her bedroom. She didn't want to have to go anywhere where she'd have to make small talk with people who were practically strangers. All she wanted to do was stay safe in her room, surrounded by her horse collections, photos, and riding books.

Looking at her wall, she caught a glimpse of her favorite poster, one that she'd gotten free in a bag of horse treats she'd bought for Sterling. It was a blurred, artistic shot of an eventer riding a small, scrappy horse. The pair was negotiating a huge picnic table jump with an enormous spread. Kaitlin had studied it countless times, wishing she knew who the gutsy horse was and wishing she had the rider's form over fences. For a few seconds she considered the plans she'd made to fire up the DVD player and watch *Eventing Greats*. Instead she stretched her sore muscles and stood up.

Walking over to her closet mirror, Kaitlin took a long look at herself. She was still wearing her dirty breeches and her *My Horse Rocks!* T-shirt. Her hair was flattened down from her helmet, her nose was sunburned, and her eyes looked tired. Her hands were stained with the bright purple thrush medicine she'd put on Bouncer earlier in the afternoon.

She had been working too hard, and it showed. Sam and Parker were right. It was time to have fun. It was time to look carefree and happy, the way Alicia did.

Forty-five minutes later, Kaitlin was showered and dressed in new black pants and a soft pink sweater that she'd never worn before. Her hair was swept up in a way that framed her oval face. She'd applied a little mascara to set off her blue eyes and touched her lips with a berry-colored gloss. Though she couldn't do much about her ragged nails, at least they were clean. She looked and felt like a new person.

"I'm going to Michaela Parsons's house," she called to her parents. They were sitting in the den playing a board game with her little sisters.

Kaitlin's dad didn't look up from the game. "Look who's going out! Well, well! Just be back by eleven."

Her mom, however, put down her game pieces and looked closely at Kaitlin. "Where did you say you were going?" she asked.

"Michaela Parsons's house. You know, the sweet-sixteen party," Kaitlin said. "See you later."

Kaitlin had just opened the front door when her mom appeared in the hallway. "I thought you didn't want to go," Mrs. Boyce said, looking puzzled but pleased.

"Changed my mind," Kaitlin replied.

"But you didn't RSVP, and you can't go wearing pants," her mom protested. "What about that sweet dress you wore to—"

"Really, Mom, it's okay," Kaitlin said, trying not to sound impatient. "Things aren't that formal anymore. People wear pants all the time to sweet sixteens. Some even wear jeans."

"Not when I was a girl, they didn't," Mrs. Boyce replied crisply.

Kaitlin tried to change the subject. "I promise I won't be late. I've got my cell phone with me."

Whew, Kaitlin thought as she stepped out the door and started down the street. For a few seconds there it had really looked as though her mother was going to insist that she wear the dress she'd worn to her cousin's wedding the month before. It was hard enough as it was to show up at a party when she hardly knew anyone. The last thing she needed was to be overdressed as well.

As she neared Michaela's house and heard the music spill out onto the street, she thought about turning around and going home. Not for the first time she considered how fearless she was on the back of a horse tearing across a cross-country course at over twenty miles per hour, but how fearful she was sitting in a roomful of near strangers.

If only Melanie or Christina or someone I knew were here, Kaitlin thought desperately, feeling an urge to chew on her nails. *If only this were an exhibitors' party and there were horse people to talk with.*

But then Kaitlin straightened her shoulders resolutely. Tonight she was going to avoid talking about horses. She was going to have fun.

"Even if it kills me," Kaitlin whispered under her breath as she started up the brick walkway leading to the Parsonses' giant Tudor-style mansion.

To the right of the front door, Kaitlin saw Madison and

Alicia huddled with a group of girls whom Kaitlin vaguely recognized from school. They were next to a pair of giant stone lions decorated with sunglasses and baseball caps.

Good. At least I know someone here. Sort of, anyway. Kaitlin took a deep breath and waved eagerly, as if the girls were all her best friends.

One of the girls peered at her curiously. "Your name's Kaitlin, right?" she asked. "I'm Danielle. You're in my English class, aren't you?"

"I think so," Kaitlin replied, though she wasn't sure. She tended to look at school as something to be endured till she was free to leave and race over to Whisperwood. As a result, she really didn't look closely at her fellow classmates and had no idea who most of them were.

"Well, Kaitlin, let me introduce you to my newest boyfriend, Leo," said Danielle with mock seriousness, putting her arm around one of the stone lions. "Aren't his shades fabulous?"

Kaitlin stood silently, unable to think of a snappy comeback. She had never been good at joking around with people she didn't know.

"He's *my* boyfriend," called out Michaela, rushing over to the lion. "I'm the birthday girl, after all! That means I call the shots." She glanced curiously at Kaitlin. "Glad you could come," she said politely.

Kaitlin was suddenly conscious that she hadn't brought

a birthday present, and she could feel her face heat up.

"Happy birthday, Michaela," she said shyly. "I, um . . . didn't bring you a present. . . ."

Michaela didn't appear to notice. She turned to flirt with a cute blond guy who came up the walk while Kaitlin stood there awkwardly. The guy glanced briefly at Kaitlin before turning back to give Michaela a wrapped present.

Here goes, Kaitlin thought, steeling herself. She walked through the front door, her heart pounding in time to the music blasting through the amplifiers. She paused in the entryway, feeling more nervous as she saw how filled the house was. Guys and girls were everywhere, talking and laughing. A few people danced in the living room, and through the picture window, Kaitlin saw a number of couples dancing outside on the terrace as well.

Okay, you're here. Now start having fun, Kaitlin ordered herself. She wandered over to the fireplace and stood in front of the flames for a few seconds.

What am I supposed to do now? she wondered. *Just walk up to some guy who's drool-on-my-shoes cute and ask him to dance?* The thought of doing something so daring made her breathless. She wondered if she should head over toward Madison, who was now standing with her friends next to a life-size cardboard cutout of James Dean, and join in the conversation. But she dismissed that thought immediately. Madison would probably ignore her.

Finally Kaitlin made her way over to a bowl of popcorn sitting on a coffee table, and plopped down on the sofa. She was glad that the popcorn gave her something to do, a sort of reason to be there. She sat there in silence for the next half hour, slowly munching kernels, watching everyone around her.

I should have stayed home and watched the tape, she thought glumly, licking her buttery fingers and scowling at how ugly her hands were. She glanced enviously at the girls around her who had manicured nails in bright colors.

Where do they get the time to do that? she wondered.

Suddenly she was conscious that someone had collapsed into the sofa next to her. It was Michaela.

"Omigosh," Michaela said, turning toward Kaitlin and laughing animatedly. "I've already been asked to dance six times tonight, not counting Leo the stone lion, and I've had two guys ask me to go out with them. If I'd known turning sixteen would be this much fun, I'd have done it a long time ago," she joked.

Kaitlin forced a smile. She'd just turned seventeen, and she hadn't been asked out once. Not that she'd ever thought about it—or cared. But now, looking at Michaela's lit-up face, she found herself wondering what she'd missed out on.

"Of course, it's exhausting to be in such demand," added Michaela.

"I wouldn't know," Kaitlin said without thinking. Instantly she clapped her hand over her mouth.

Boyce, did you come here to stage your own pity party? she scolded herself.

"Here," Michaela said, suddenly taking off her crystal sweet-sixteen tiara. "You wear this. You look like you need it."

Kaitlin put up her hands to block Michaela, who was trying to put the shiny crown on her head. "No, no, that's okay, really," she said, feeling embarrassed. *Do I really seem that pathetic?* She forced herself to smile even wider.

Michaela ignored her protests and placed the tiara on her. "Never mess with the princess. Hey," she said, grabbing the cute blond guy Kaitlin had seen at the door, who was walking in front of the couch. "I hereby command you to dance with this girl." The guy stopped and gave Kaitlin a full dose of his green eyes, which were the color of sea glass.

He looks familiar, Kaitlin thought before she realized what Michaela had said to him.

"If the birthday girl wishes it," the guy said, turning toward Michaela and bowing slightly. Then he jerked Kaitlin to her feet so quickly she didn't know what was happening.

"Her name's Kaitlin. She rides horses," Michaela said politely before standing up and rushing off.

"Really, you don't have to dance with me," Kaitlin

mumbled to the guy, trying to free her hand. She wished she could sink into the parquet floor and just disappear. She'd been an idiot to come to a party where everyone else seemed to have the ability to socialize that she'd never had.

"Of course I do," the guy said, regarding her with a grin as he half dragged her through the living room toward the terrace. "You heard her. Michaela is She Who Must Be Obeyed. She told me to dance with you. That's the end of it."

In spite of herself, Kaitlin had to laugh. She allowed herself to be led onto the dance floor, and for a few seconds she stood awkwardly and watched as the guy started to dance. Soon she found herself moving in time to the music, wishing she could think of something brilliant and witty to say. But the music was so loud, Kaitlin realized that she could say anything and it probably wouldn't matter.

"So how long have you known Michaela?" she asked the guy, thrilled that she had managed to speak at all.

He held up two fingers, which Kaitlin took to mean two years. "We met in Florida, and both ended up moving to Lexington at the same time. Our folks work for the same TV station," he called out.

Kaitlin studied his face while they continued dancing. She found herself aching to reach over and push back a lock of blond hair that had fallen across his forehead.

"So you ride horses?" the guy asked.

Kaitlin nodded.

"I've ridden a few myself," the guy said just as the music started to get louder.

Kaitlin looked up sharply. *He's a rider!* she thought, her heart leaping. She looked at him, feeling herself drawn to him even more. *If only the music weren't so loud.* She wanted to ask him where he rode and what style of riding he preferred. Maybe he was an eventer!

Kaitlin closed her eyes and tried to forget everything but the scent of his aftershave.

4

When the dance ended, the mysterious guy led Kaitlin back toward the sofa.

"This seat taken?" he asked, gesturing to the spot next to where she'd been sitting.

Kaitlin couldn't believe her good luck. He wasn't going to take off just because the dance was over, like other guys she'd danced with usually did. Unable to utter a word, she shook her head and unconsciously bit her fingernail.

I wish I could figure out where I've seen him before, she thought, stealing a glance at the guy's perfect profile.

"Well, save it for me while I go get us some sodas," he said, disappearing into the crowd.

Kaitlin stopped biting her nail and reached up to

straighten Michaela's tiara on her head. She wanted to hug herself with happiness. The cute guy was getting her a soda, and he wanted to sit with her!

Must be the power of the lucky tiara, she thought, grinning like an idiot.

She sat there waiting for what seemed like forever. After a while, she wondered if he'd forgotten all about her.

Oh, well, Kaitlin thought, trying not to feel disappointed. It had seemed too good to be true. She'd never been the type to attract guys. She began debating whether she ought to slip out and go home. Just as she was about to stand up to leave, she saw the guy leaning against the kitchen door, talking with two girls. They were both incredibly pretty, and they didn't seem to be at a loss for conversation.

He probably likes girls who are more outgoing, Kaitlin thought. She watched him for a few seconds, biting her lip and wishing she'd never come to the party. It wasn't worth feeling crummy over some guy whose name she didn't even know.

Suddenly he caught her eye and walked across the room.

"Sorry. I got cornered by some of my friends," the guy said, handing her a soda and sitting down next to her. "Where were we? Oh, yeah, getting to know each other. You're an eventer, right? The kind that goes screaming over huge logs and things."

Kaitlin almost choked on her soda. "How do you know that?" she gasped.

The guy grinned and shrugged. "Psychic, I guess."

Kaitlin was about to ask him about his riding, but just then the band started playing a familiar song.

"Pegasus's newest," the guy said, jumping up and grabbing Kaitlin's hand. "Want to dance some more?"

"Sure," Kaitlin agreed happily. "This is one of my favorite new songs. A friend of mine—her horse won the Kentucky Derby—she's dating a guy from Pegasus." Instantly, she felt foolish for having indulged in some name-dropping. If only she weren't such a klutz when it came to talking with people she didn't know.

But the guy merely nodded. "Melanie Graham. She goes out with Jazz Taylor, right?"

"You seem to have the 411 on everything," Kaitlin murmured. She wished she knew as much about this cute stranger as he seemed to know about her. He'd asked about eventing. He knew who Melanie Graham was. He definitely was involved in horses in some way, she thought.

When the dance was over, she finally asked his name.

"Connor Hamilton," he said. "And you're Kaitlin Boyce, you're seventeen, and you go to Henry Clay."

"Yeah," Kaitlin replied. "You sure know a lot about me. How?"

Connor shoved his hands into his pockets and rocked

from side to side, like a little boy caught doing something wrong. "All right," he said, grinning again. "It's confession time. When I saw you come in, I was trying to place you. Then later, you were sitting here and I thought you were really pretty. I asked Michaela who you were and she filled me in. She said she'd figure out a way for me to meet you. I was kind of nervous, but I decided to let Michaela work her magic."

Kaitlin ducked her head so he wouldn't see how psyched she was. Connor had been nervous, too! Wow, so she wasn't the only one in the world. And look how he'd pushed past his nervousness to go meet her.

You could learn something from him, she told herself.

Just as Kaitlin started to ask him where he rode, a group of guys and girls walked over to him. *Theater club types,* Kaitlin realized immediately. They didn't seem to notice that Kaitlin was there. They simply started to talk with him about the upcoming school play, and he joined in eagerly.

For a second she felt disappointed that Connor's attention was now elsewhere. But when she saw him scoot closer to be next to her and turn to look at her every so often, she relaxed.

So what if he isn't talking with me? Kaitlin told herself. Actually, she realized, it was easier to listen in than to try to think up things to say.

As the conversation went on, Kaitlin gathered that Connor had a big role in the play, but she had no idea which play it was. She made a mental note to find out and ask him about it. Now, however, didn't seem to be the time. She knew nothing about theater, and Connor and his friends seemed to speak a language she didn't know at all. But she didn't care. It was enough to watch his eyes dance as he told his stories and to see how he held the attention of everyone in the group.

I wonder what that would feel like, Kaitlin found herself thinking as the evening went on. Being shy herself, Kaitlin envied those who could be totally at ease in the spotlight. Several times Connor jumped up to greet people, and once or twice he asked another girl to dance. But he always returned to Kaitlin's side.

Too soon, she noticed her watch. It was nearing eleven.

She reluctantly removed her hand from his grasp, hoping he hadn't felt her ragged fingernails. "It was nice meeting you," she said to Connor.

Connor jumped to his feet. "You're leaving already?" He gestured to the terrace. "One last dance?"

"Can't," Kaitlin said. "I promised my parents I'd be back at eleven."

"Too bad," Connor said. "I'll walk you out."

As she started toward the door Kaitlin bit the inside of her cheek so she wouldn't start grinning again. Already her face hurt because she'd been smiling all night. As she walked past the kitchen, she saw Michaela.

"Gotta return the tiara," she said to Connor, ready to duck into the kitchen. But she stopped when she realized Michaela was busy flirting with a football player.

Kaitlin turned around, her cheeks flaming. "Guess I'll return it some other time," she mumbled.

Connor's eyes sparkled. "I doubt she's missing it much right now, and anyway, it looks better on you."

Kaitlin giggled as though she was used to such compliments, but inside she was exploding with happiness. All too soon, this night was going to end, and she'd be going home, back to being the same old shy Kaitlin who thought only about horses.

As she stepped out onto the front porch, she glanced at Leo the stone lion, who was now sporting a basketball jersey as well as his shades and baseball cap. For a split second Kaitlin thought about placing the tiara on top of his hat. But then she decided against it. She'd keep the sparkly crown so that she'd have something to remember Connor by.

"Good night," Kaitlin said, turning toward Connor. She'd never met a guy quite like him before. Gazing into his amazing sea-glass-colored eyes, she swallowed hard. She found herself trying to memorize his face. It would probably be the last time she saw him this close.

"Well, see ya around," Connor said abruptly.

Kaitlin turned and started walking into the night. Just as she reached the sidewalk, she heard hurried footsteps.

She turned just as Connor thrust a piece of paper into her hand.

"My e-mail address and AIM name," he said. "Can I IM you sometime?"

"Sure," Kaitlin said happily, shoving it into her purse without looking at it. She told him her screen name and e-mail address and turned to go home.

I wonder if he'll remember it, she thought, hurrying down the lamplit street.

The next morning Kaitlin glanced out the window at the puffy clouds chasing across a brilliant blue sky and felt like whooping. It was a perfect day for galloping over the cross-country course. She glanced at her eventing poster and briefly ran her finger over the horse that was pictured in it. She couldn't get over how he jumped the enormous obstacle with room to spare, even though he was so small.

Closing her eyes, she imagined herself taking Sterling over that fence, rocketing on to Capability's Cutting at Burghley and then on to the Rosette just before the finish. Automatically she reached for her breeches and boots. She couldn't wait to saddle up and take Sterling over Whisperwood's course. Suddenly the memory of what had happened to the mare came flooding back. At least for now, Sterling was lame.

No riding today—or for the next few days, she thought darkly. Her mood immediately plunged. She tossed her breeches back over her chair with more force than was necessary.

"Now what'll I do all day?" Kaitlin muttered. Without riding, the hours seemed to stretch out endlessly before her. Sure, she'd go to Whisperwood first thing and check on Sterling, but after that? She wrinkled her nose as she considered the bleak prospect of a boring weekend.

She could always get an early start on her English paper on the works of Ralph Waldo Emerson. *Ugh!* she thought immediately. Or maybe she could clean tack, roll bandages, and help out Sam and Parker in a zillion different ways. But somehow that didn't seem as appealing to her as it normally would have. She flopped back against her pillows and gazed at the tiara now sitting on top of her Whisperwood fleece jacket.

Kaitlin reached over and flicked on the computer sitting on her desk. The first thing she saw was the new message sign blinking in her mailbox. One of the messages was from someone she didn't recognize.

"Who do I know with that screen name?" she asked, perplexed. For a second, she considered deleting the message. After all, she'd heard all the lectures about Internet safety. But something reckless in her made her shrug and double-click instead.

Pop quiz for you, she read as she glanced at the screen. *"A horse, a horse, my kingdom for a horse!" Who wrote it?*

Kaitlin frowned. The words sounded familiar. Who wrote them? And who had sent her this so-called pop quiz anyway? She sat at her desk for a few moments, repeating the quotation. She'd read it somewhere, but where? Kaitlin bit her nail while she racked her memory. Finally she picked up her English book and flipped through it, looking for clues. Suddenly it came to her: William Shakespeare.

"Richard III," she said triumphantly. She had read part of the play in her English class in September. Mentally picturing her English class, she suddenly placed where she'd seen Connor before. He sat in the back of the room.

He sent me the pop quiz! Kaitlin thought. *He remembered my e-mail address!*

Kaitlin typed back, *Shakespeare*—Richard III. *That was easy.* Then she added one of her favorite horse quotes: *"The outside of a horse is good for the inside of man." Your turn. Who wrote this?* Hitting the send button, she sent it zinging.

"Connor likes horses, and he likes me too!" Kaitlin said to her reflection in the mirror as she brushed her hair.

"You're awfully happy this morning," her mom greeted her when Katlin came into the kitchen a few minutes later.

"Mmm," Kaitlin said noncommittally, reaching for a crisp apple from the bowl on the table. She wasn't quite

ready to mention Connor to her mom—not yet, anyway.

"You're not wearing riding clothes," said ten-year-old Jordan, who was eyeing her suspiciously.

Her other sister, Lindy, who was a year older, was more direct. "What gives?"

Kaitlin bit into her apple. "Sterling's off for a few days. Front leg problem," she said. She was amazed at how calm she sounded. Just the day before, it had seemed like the worst thing ever. This morning it didn't seem so horrible. Sterling just needed to rest up, that was all. "Of course, I still have to go to the barn and groom her and everything," Kaitlin added.

"Are you going to ride another horse while Sterling's off?" her mom asked.

Kaitlin nodded. "Yeah, if Sam has any horses to spare. But maybe I won't be that lucky."

"Uh-oh. Kaitlin always goes berserk when she can't ride." Jordan's eyes grew wide.

Kaitlin ruffled Jordan's curly hair. "No, I don't. Anyway, it's just for a couple of days," she said, more to herself than to her little sister.

Slipping out the door, she jumped into the dented old car that Parker sometimes teased her about. It was the one her mom had driven since her college days and it was pretty beaten up, but Kaitlin didn't care. It was hers now, and she was so thrilled to have her own car that it didn't matter how it looked. Taking the wheel, she turned the key in the ignition and headed toward Whisperwood. When she snapped on the radio and heard the Pegasus tune she'd danced to the night before, she found her thoughts turning to Connor and his amazing eyes.

"Quit being a complete freak," she told herself as she turned into Whisperwood's driveway. "He's just a guy."

"Oh, Kaitlin, there you are," Sam said as Kaitlin passed the barn office. "Good news. There's absolutely no heat or swelling this morning, and Sterling's standing squarely, just the way she should be."

"That's great," Kaitlin said, beaming as she thought of Connor's e-mailed message.

"I knew you'd be happy. Of course, we'll play it safe and rest her like Dr. Tanner said, but I thought you'd be glad to know it's almost as if nothing had happened," said Sam. "At this point, I'm guessing maybe she just got trimmed too short when the farrier came. Or maybe she got a hot nail or something."

Kaitlin nodded absently and continued down the barn aisle.

"Penny's mom called to cancel her lesson," Sam called after her. "Seems that she's got the stomach flu, poor kid. I put you down to ride Chili since she won't be here."

Ride Chili? Kaitlin stopped in her tracks. She did not want to ride a stubborn kid's pony. She wanted to forget her riding worries and be happy for a while. Was that such a crime?

"Okay if I don't?" Kaitlin said, taking a deep breath and turning to face Sam.

Sam regarded Kaitlin, then looked back down at her riding schedule. "Well, okay, I guess. Let's see . . . you're getting too tall to school Jelly Roll, Justin's pretty well worn out Bouncer, and Snicker and Scooter are going to be used in lessons today, so that really only leaves—"

"I guess maybe I just want to take a break today," Kaitlin said softly. "Just for the next few days."

"There's no need to lose your muscle tone just because—" Sam started to say. But she broke off in midsentence and simply looked at Kaitlin. Kaitlin lowered her head and stared at her paddock boots. She stood there for a moment, feeling like she should try to explain, but finally she let out a breath and walked on.

It's not like it's the end of the world if I don't ride until Sterling gets better, Kaitlin thought defensively as she neared her mare's stall. *It's just a couple of days, that's all.*

She smiled when she heard Sterling's nickered greeting. Standing in front of Sterling's stall, Kaitlin watched the horse almost unseeingly as she turned back to take another mouthful of green hay.

Sterling, I met the most unbelievable guy, Kaitlin wanted to say. Instead, she swallowed the words and let her eyes trail

56

down to the mare's left fore, pleased that Sterling wasn't appearing to favor any of her legs more than the others.

Kaitlin had just opened the stall door when she saw Alicia emerging from Scooter's stall, which was next to Sterling's.

"Hi," Alicia said to Kaitlin. She turned to tug on Scooter's lead and muttered crossly, "Come on, you big lug. I was out late last night, I'm tired, and I definitely don't need this right now."

"Hi," Kaitlin called out to Alicia. Suddenly she wished she knew Alicia better and could ask her about Connor. Maybe Alicia could tell her more about him. There were a zillion things she was dying to know. "Fun party, huh?"

"Yeah," replied Alicia, yawning.

Kaitlin paused and began unfastening the front buckles on the part of the blanket that crossed Sterling's chest, hoping Alicia would go on.

"It's just that I'm totally zonked. I should have bailed on my lesson and slept in," Alicia said.

"I know what you mean," Kaitlin lied, just to keep the topic of the party afloat a bit longer. She wasn't tired in the least. In fact, thinking about Connor pumped her so full of energy, she could hardly stand still long enough to unbuckle the rest of the surcingles on Sterling's blanket.

Alicia stopped in front of Sterling's stall. "Madison's not too happy, you know. We heard about you and Connor," she stated, her eyes seeming to gleam in the dim light of the barn.

Kaitlin looked straight ahead at Sterling's dappled shoulder before turning toward Alicia. What could Alicia have heard about her and Connor? What was there to hear?

"What do you mean?" Kaitlin asked, trying to keep her voice as free of expression as possible.

Alicia shrugged. "Well, let's just say she can't figure out what Connor was thinking," she said as she jerked Scooter's lead. "But anyway, it's not a big deal."

Kaitlin heard Scooter's metal shoes ring out as Alicia led him down the concrete barn aisle. Did Madison like Connor? Was she stepping on Madison's toes?

"People are so weird," Kaitlin murmured to Sterling. "Now you see why I prefer horses."

Sterling snorted and thrust her nose under Kaitlin's arm.

"Oh, Sterling," Kaitlin said, smoothing her forelock. "You and I are pals forever, right?"

She smiled fondly at her horse before taking the blanket to hang out on the blanket rail.

When Sterling finished eating, Kaitlin took her to the cross ties for a grooming. She tried to block out the sounds of the students bustling around her. She had just started combing Sterling's thick tail when a brush zinged past her head. Looking up, Kaitlin saw that it was Justin who had fired the missile.

"Sorry, Kaitlin," he said, coloring furiously. "I meant to hit Lisa."

"You'll be in big trouble if Parker or Sam catches you throwing brushes around," she snapped.

"Grouch!" Justin called back, sticking his tongue out at her.

Kaitlin glared at him and went back to grooming Sterling. While she worked, she tried to picture Connor's face. She imagined herself brushing back that lock of hair the way she'd wanted to the night before. As she cleaned out Sterling's hooves, she found herself wondering whether he'd read her e-mail yet. Maybe he'd already sent her another one! She tried to push her worry over the Madison issue behind her.

The thought made her heart race, and she finished up Sterling's grooming session quickly.

"Sorry, girl, no cross-country today," she told her mare absently as she put her back into her stall. Sterling looked at her with deep, liquid brown eyes.

"Stop it," Kaitlin said. "Don't you think I feel bad enough?" She picked up her grooming box and sighed.

"Kaitlin, where are the filis irons?" Morgan Alexander pounced on her the second she stepped into the tack room to put away her grooming box.

"I have absolutely no idea," Kaitlin said.

"No idea?" Morgan asked. He looked shocked. "But you always know where everything is."

Kaitlin shook her head and walked out of the tack room.

Wow. Answer Girl just blew her reputation! Kaitlin thought. *And guess what? It feels good!*

Just then Sam appeared in the doorway. "Kaitlin, since you're not doing anything, would you mind packing the tack I'm donating in this box so I can label it and send it off to the Thoroughbred Retirement Foundation?"

Kaitlin nodded automatically. While she stuffed the tack into the cardboard carton, however, she felt herself filling with resentment. She was tired of being asked to do this and do that. All she wanted was to go somewhere and think about the interesting new guy she'd just met.

I've got to get away from this place, she thought suddenly.

Minutes later, Kaitlin did something she'd never done before: left Whisperwood without riding—and without saying good-bye to anyone. All she could think about was whether she'd find a new e-mail from Connor when she got back home!

5

On Wednesday, when Kaitlin arrived at the barn, she saw Dr. Tanner standing outside Sterling's stall talking with Sam.

"Is everything okay?" she asked anxiously while hurrying over to the stall.

Sam grinned and nodded. "Oh, you're here. I was going to call you if you didn't show up. Dr. Tanner here has given Sterling the green light," she said. "You can ride this afternoon."

"That's great," Kaitlin replied, grinning at Sam, then turned to thank the vet.

At least one good thing had happened in the last couple of days, Kaitlin thought as she placed Sterling's halter over her head. She had thought that by staying away from Whisperwood, somehow she'd magically have fun. But she hadn't. She'd been bored, for one thing. And for another, she hadn't seen Connor at school or heard from him, either.

"He's got the stomach flu," Michaela had told Kaitlin during lunch period, when Kaitlin had finally worked up the courage to ask where he was.

Kaitlin had walked away quickly, not wanting Michaela to think she was overly concerned about Connor's whereabouts. She debated sending him another e-mail but decided against it. She didn't know much about guys, but it didn't seem smart to have him think she was stalking him or anything.

Now she tacked up Sterling absently, wondering if maybe she'd dreamed the whole scenario on Saturday night.

When Kaitlin settled into her saddle, she expected to feel a surge of relief at finally being back on Sterling and ready to work. Instead, she felt awkward, as if her saddle had changed shape and now didn't fit quite right.

Riding to the outdoor arena, she saw that it was Sam and not Parker waiting to give her her lesson.

"Where's Parker?" she asked.

"I thought he told you. He flew to New Jersey to a dressage clinic with Dr. Leidgens," Sam replied. "Dr. Leidgens is from Germany, and he's a wizard at dressage. Parker's one lucky guy."

Kaitlin scanned her brain. If Parker had mentioned the clinic to her, she didn't remember it.

Sam grinned. "Well, anyway, I'm teaching you this week."

"Cool," Kaitlin said. But she groaned inwardly. While Parker certainly worked her hard during a lesson, Sam definitely was more of a taskmaster. Kaitlin hoped that she'd get lucky and Sam would go lightly since Sterling had been off for a few days.

"Let's take it easy on Sterling this afternoon," Sam said, as if reading Kaitlin's mind. "I don't want to push it. I want to make sure she stays good and sound for Deep Woods."

Taking it easy works for me, Kaitlin thought.

Forty-five minutes later, Kaitlin rode tiredly from the ring. If she had thought Sam meant that by taking it easy on Sterling she'd also be taking it easy on Kaitlin, she'd been badly mistaken. Sam made Kaitlin fold her irons over and ride without stirrups the entire lesson. Riding without stirrups was tough enough for anyone, let alone someone who hadn't ridden in days. Now every muscle screamed. When Kaitlin jumped down from her saddle, her legs felt weak and even shook for a few seconds.

She walked Sterling over to the wash racks and hosed down her legs, not daring to complain. Sam would only tell her that she should have ridden Chili when she'd had the chance.

The next day was more of the same, only this time Sam let Kaitlin pick up her irons partway through her flat lesson.

"See how riding without stirrups can help? You're sitting more evenly now," Sam observed after her lesson.

Big whoop, thought Kaitlin irritably. She climbed down from Sterling's back and pulled the reins over her head, trying to ignore the pain in her back and legs. To get her mind off her soreness while she walked back toward the barn with Sam, she thought instead about Connor's smile and about the smell of his aftershave when they'd danced together.

Maybe today he's feeling better and he'll e-mail me, she thought, brightening.

"So we'll be back to full work by this weekend," she vaguely heard Sam say.

"Huh?" Kaitlin said, jerking herself to the present.

"I said we'll be back to full work by this weekend," Sam repeated. "I was worried that we were cutting it close, but we'll have time to prepare for Deep Woods. I think you'll be fine."

"Yeah, sure, whatever," Kaitlin replied absently.

"You okay?" Sam asked, looking at her closely as they approached the barn.

"Yeah, why?" Kaitlin asked, reaching up to pat Sterling's neck.

"Nothing. You just seem distracted lately, that's all," Sam murmured. She rubbed her lower back.

"I'm not distracted," Kaitlin said. "I'm just so relieved that Sterling's okay, I guess I'm not that worked up about the trial anymore."

"Hmmm," Sam said. "It's good not to be too nervous, but you still want to be on your toes."

Kaitlin simply nodded.

Turning, Sam called out, "See you tomorrow. If all goes well with Sterling, we'll pop over a few cross-country fences."

Normally the word *cross-country* would have sent a thrill down Kaitlin's spine, but this day it didn't do anything for her. She was far more interested in whether there'd be an e-mail waiting for her when she got home.

The next day at school, Kaitlin felt her heart slam into her chest when she saw Connor walk into her English classroom. Though he looked slightly pale, he sauntered in, smiling and waving at his friends. He was wearing a green sweater that set off his blond hair.

Kaitlin tried to catch his eye, taking in his well-built frame and trying not to stare. Suddenly she realized that he hadn't looked her way at all.

He's forgotten all about me! She was surprised at how much that hurt. Swiftly she glanced at the floor and tried to choke down her disappointment as he walked past her desk.

"Churchill," he whispered suddenly, almost in her ear.

"Huh?" she said. Then it hit her—he was answering her e-mail pop quiz. He was telling her that Churchill was the one who'd said "The outside of a horse is good for the inside of man."

"Gotcha," Connor said devilishly while he sat down.

Kaitlin slid down in her seat, her cheeks heating up and her nerves zinging. Twice during class, she pretended to get something out of her backpack hanging on the back of her chair so that she could steal a peek at Connor. Both times he was looking at her. Once he grinned, displaying a row of perfect white teeth.

He looks like a model or something, Kaitlin thought, looking away again.

When the bell rang, Connor came right over to her.

"I'm glad you recovered from the flu," Kaitlin said, hoping she didn't sound as eager as she felt.

Connor nodded. "Me too. Believe me, it wasn't pretty."

Kaitlin stood and stuffed her books in her backpack. She was glad when Connor fell in beside her and started walking her down the hall.

"The drama club is having a barbecue on Sunday afternoon," he said while they made their way through the throng of students. "Want to go with me?"

66

Kaitlin nodded and clutched her backpack straps. He hadn't forgotten about her after all! The thought made her so happy, she felt slightly dizzy.

That afternoon at Whisperwood, Kaitlin saddled Sterling dreamily and rode into the outdoor arena.

"Why the goofy smile?" Parker asked, walking up to her and stroking Sterling's nose. "Have you been sitting in the tack room inhaling leather or something?"

Kaitlin blinked and immediately stopped smiling. "Ha ha. You're a riot. What are you doing here, anyway?" she sputtered. "I thought you were off at some big-deal dressage clinic."

"I *was*," Parker said. "But Dr. Leidgens got sick, so he canceled the rest of the clinic. And here I am, back on the farm."

"Well, you'd better not get sick and then pass on any nasty bug to me." She shivered at the thought of getting sick and having to miss the barbecue.

"Don't worry. I make it a point never to let any germs hitch a free ride on me," Parker replied. "Anyway, you can't get sick."

Kaitlin looked up, wondering how he'd guessed what she'd been thinking.

Parker looked at her. "You've got a silver statuette to win at Deep Woods."

"Oh, yeah, that," Kaitlin said, heaving a sigh.

"Ready to jump?" Parker added, giving her a look and gesturing to the stadium jump course he'd set up in the outdoor arena.

"I thought we were going to go cross-country today," Kaitlin said. She frowned and tugged at the chin strap on her helmet.

"Sam told me that you might be better working over fences in the ring," Parker said.

"Why?" Kaitlin was mystified.

Parker shrugged. "Does it matter?" He walked over to a combination and started pacing off the distances between the elements.

"It matters to me," Kaitlin said with an edge in her voice.

"Maybe it's because the Olympic committee's decided to do away with roads and tracks at the Olympics, and they're probably going to make stadium jumping tougher. You know, to compensate," Parker said, talking in a rush and not meeting Kaitlin's eyes. "So Sam figures they'll amp up the stadium jumping at Deep Woods, and she wants you to be ready."

Kaitlin had a feeling that Parker was covering up the real reason Sam had changed the lesson around.

Oh, well, Kaitlin thought, starting out at a working walk. *No biggie*. She didn't feel like having to gear up for the cross-country fences anyway. Amped up or not, these stadium jumps still looked easy. She could keep thinking about Connor while she popped over them.

Big mistake. She'd just cantered over a couple of verticals and had started for the combination when she found herself on the other side of the first element—on the ground!

"What happened?" she asked, sitting up.

Parker scooted over to catch Sterling, who'd stopped a few feet away and was now looking at Kaitlin balefully.

"You tell me," he replied.

Kaitlin spat out some dirt and stood. "I don't know," she said.

"You took your eye off the ball," Parker said, giving her a leg up.

"Whatever that means," groused Kaitlin.

"Baseball saying," Parker replied lightly. "It means you weren't focusing. These are tight turns. You can't come out here and daydream."

"Okay, okay. I'll focus," Kaitlin replied, mounting again and picking up the reins.

Kaitlin tried to keep her mind on her fences, but she found herself wondering what she'd wear to the barbecue. She missed several distances, but Sterling soldiered on bravely anyway.

"Jeez, do you realize how lucky you are?" Parker said

after the plank at the far corner. "You absolutely buried Sterling, and she still came through for you."

"I know, I know," Kaitlin whimpered.

"That's enough for today," Parker finally said.

"Okay," Kaitlin said in a weak voice.

"*Okay?*" Parker asked incredulously. "No 'Just one more jump, pleeeeeeze, Parker,' like usual?"

"No," Kaitlin said quietly. She studied Parker's blue polo shirt. *Blue*, she thought. *That's the color I'll wear!*

Parker regarded her for a moment before reaching down and picking up a dirt clod.

"One week till Deep Woods. Better come armed and dangerous," he said sternly.

Kaitlin nodded. "Armed and dangerous," she replied, saluting him.

Parker studied the dirt clod intently, then turned to look into her eyes. His normally smoky gray eyes now were cool and steely. "Out with it, Boyce. There's something on your mind, and you know it. "

Kaitlin tried to give him her most innocent look. "There's nothing on my mind," she shot back.

Parker tossed the dirt clod and wiped his hands on his breeches. "Horses don't lie," he said quietly. "Sam told me you haven't been yourself these last few days, and I didn't believe it. But I can tell by looking at the way Sterling goes that Sam was right. "

"You're the one who's been inhaling leather, Parker Townsend," Kaitlin said. "Nothing's on my mind."

"Deny all you want," Parker replied. "But I can tell you one thing—if you don't get yourself back together, and quickly, you're going to have a real accident! And not the kind that only takes a few days to heal from, either."

With that, he walked off, leaving a shocked Kaitlin alone in the center of the ring.

6

"FORGET YOU, PARKER TOWNSEND!" KAITLIN SPAT IN THE general direction of Parker's back. "I can't wait till you go off to train for the Olympics. Maybe this time I'll get lucky, and you'll never come back!"

She dismounted, automatically loosening Sterling's girth and running up her irons. A cool wind was now starting up, and it cut through her fleece, causing her to shiver. But she stood for a long while, staring at Whisperwood's grounds and feeling her stomach churn. She looked upstairs at the cozy little house where just recently she'd helped Christina and her mom, Ashleigh Griffen, get the nursery ready for Sam's babies. The light was on in the family room, a place where she'd gathered with her friends many times to celebrate horse-show victories as well as other happy events.

This place had meant so much to her for the last few years. Now it was doing nothing but causing her to feel bad.

Why does everyone feel like they need to tell me what to do all the time? Kaitlin thought, tears prickling at the back of her eyes. *Especially Parker and Sam. Do this. Do that. Focus. Relax. Have fun. Get to work. Stop working and take it easy. You're taking it a little too easy.*

After grooming Sterling and putting her away, Kaitlin jumped into her car, Parker's words still ringing in her ears. When she arrived home, she went straight to her room and closed her door, making no move to get up when Jordan started knocking on it.

"Come play softball with me, Kaitlin!" called Jordan plaintively.

"Go away and play with Lindy," she said crossly, kicking off her paddock boots.

"I can't," Jordan replied. "Lindy's off somewhere, pouting. You play with me."

Kaitlin turned on her portable CD player and cranked up the volume. Flopping onto her bed, she found herself looking straight at her poster. Glancing at it reminded her of eventing—the last thing she needed just then. Without thinking, she jumped up, ripped the poster off the wall, and wadded it up. She tossed it in the general direction of her wastebasket and stamped back to her bed.

She wished she had someone to call. It was Friday night. She ought to be having fun. Parker and Sam had told her so themselves. Instead, she was sitting in her room stewing about—what else?—horses.

Kaitlin, you need to start acting like a normal girl! she told herself fiercely. Then it occurred to her that she *was* acting like a normal girl. She was interested in a nice guy, and he seemed interested in her. After all, he'd asked her to a barbecue on Sunday. That was a start.

Then what? Kaitlin scratched her nose, considering what might be in the future. Was it possible that she and Connor would start going out for real? Did she have time for a boyfriend? The thought made Kaitlin sit up and take off her headphones. Already she was pushed for hours in her day, what with school and her riding schedule. She would only be more crunched if she started to win at her preliminary events and began stepping up to the advanced level. She'd be traveling with Sterling all over Kentucky— and maybe out of state as well.

Melanie and Christina have boyfriends, she reminded herself. *They manage to juggle careers as professional jockeys and spend time with their guys.*

But then she thought back to when Parker and Christina had broken up because of their conflicting schedules. And

Melanie and Jazz hardly seemed to spend any time together, and she'd heard somewhere that things seemed a little rocky with them lately.

This whole relationship thing sure is complicated, Kaitlin thought, settling into her pillow and feeling her eyes grow heavy.

Just before she drifted off to sleep, it occurred to her that when it got right down to it, it was the horses that made it all so complex.

Moonlight was pooling softly onto the floor through her window when Kaitlin woke hours later. A slight pinging sound penetrated Kaitlin's consciousness, and she sat up in her darkened bedroom. For a moment she didn't know what had awakened her. But then she realized that the pinging sound was coming from her computer, which she'd accidentally left on. She could see an eerie glow emanating from her monitor. An instant message! Now fully awake, Kaitlin walked over to her desk, her bare feet tingling against the cool hardwood floor.

"'What's up?'" she read as she peered at her screen.

Connor! Kaitlin thought happily. Eagerly she sat down to type a reply.

Nothing, she wrote. Then she made a face. She'd have to do better than that.

She wished she were funny and witty, the way Parker was. *No, don't think about him,* she ordered herself. *He's being a jerk.*

Closing her eyes, she found herself drifting back to Michaela's party and pictured herself dancing with Connor. He seemed to accept people as they were. She could never imagine Connor lecturing her the way Parker had.

You still there? she read when she opened her eyes.

Yes, she hastily typed in. She hoped she'd be able to keep up at least a halfway decent conversation.

You must be doing all right, she told herself approvingly a few minutes later. After all, each time she wrote something, Connor responded right away. Of course, her comments were short and to the point. Everything he wrote was elaborate and funny. It took all her concentration to think of a smooth reply. She wasn't used to chatting on the computer. Usually she managed to occasionally check her e-mails and that was it. She couldn't help thinking that it was actually lots of fun. It was better than the phone because she didn't have to talk.

"No wonder so many people around school like IMing," Kaitlin murmured wonderingly to herself as her conversation with Connor continued.

When Kaitlin happened to glance up from her screen, her jaw dropped as she saw what time it was.

How did it get to be so late? she wondered. It was past

midnight. Kaitlin studied her screen for a few seconds, amazed at how much fun it was talking with Connor—much more fun than she'd been having lately worrying about horses and hotshots who thought they had all the answers!

I've gotta go. TTYL, she typed reluctantly to Connor, and then signed off her computer.

She tossed and turned for hours, finally falling asleep near dawn.

When Kaitlin dragged herself to Whisperwood the next morning, she was conscious of the big dark circles under her eyes. Though she'd tried to cover them with some makeup left over from her cousin's wedding, she knew they were still way too visible.

Justin was the first one at the barn to see her. He came up next to her as she stood studying the message board outside Sam's office. Instead of looking at the board, he gaped at her. "Gosh, you look awful, Kaitlin. Is something wrong?"

"No," she mumbled, ducking into the office and hoping the hot pot was on. It was. She found a Styrofoam cup and pressed the hot water spigot. Just as she dunked a tea bag in her cup, Sam came in, followed by Christina, who hobbled in on her crutches.

Seeing Christina on crutches instead of on Star's back always make Kaitlin feel slightly sick. It wasn't fair that someone who loved racing so much should be stuck on the ground, giving lessons to others who could ride.

"Hi, Christina," Kaitlin said, blowing on her tea.

"Hey, Kaitlin," Christina said. She gave her a funny look, then grabbed a schedule from Sam before clomping back out of the office.

"I've never known you to be a tea drinker, Kaitlin," Sam said absently. She flipped through the phone book on her desk.

"Mmm," Kaitlin replied. She took a huge gulp from her cup, reeling as the hot liquid scalded her mouth.

Sam looked up from the phone book and studied her for a moment. "You don't look well," she said with concern in her voice. "I could have Allie ride Sterling for you if you want."

"Okay!" Kaitlin was surprised how eager she sounded. Usually she was jealous at the thought of Allie riding her beloved Sterling. But because she was tired today, it didn't matter who rode her.

After looking in on Sterling, Kaitlin jumped in her car and drove off. Maybe Connor would e-mail her or call and confirm the invitation to the barbecue. He'd never mentioned it again, so Kaitlin was beginning to wonder if he even remembered that he'd asked her. By the time she got home, she had convinced herself that Connor was totally out of her league altogether.

All that evening, she sat in front of her computer, waiting for the ping sound that meant Connor was IMing her. But it never came.

"You dork. You lost your head over some guy who's probably already asked out someone else," Kaitlin told herself sternly as she climbed into bed and pulled up her covers. She couldn't believe she'd let a guy get to her so badly. But she lay on her back for hours staring at the ceiling before falling asleep.

The sun was halfway up in the sky when Kaitlin awoke. Though it was late, she felt tired to the bone. Her eyes felt even grittier than yesterday, and the dark circles seemed to be a permanent feature on her face. As soon as she arrived at Whisperwood, she went to Sam's office and automatically made herself another cup of tea.

Sam took one look at her and said, "How about if you just hack today?" It was more a statement than a question.

She knows I'm in no shape for a lesson, Kaitlin thought.

"We'll work over some cross-country fences tomorrow afternoon," Sam added. "That okay?"

"Great," Kaitlin said, slipping out the door. She didn't want to take a chance that Sam would ask why she'd turned up late on a weekend day looking and feeling the way she did.

On her way to Sterling's stall, she passed Parker, who was thinning Black Hawke's mane in the cross ties.

"Hey, Kaitlin," he said, as though nothing had happened on Friday.

"Hi," Kaitlin said reluctantly, turning away so he wouldn't see her eyes and make one of his famous jokes.

I don't need any more comments, she thought.

Stopping in front of Sterling's stall, she watched as Sterling stood up and ambled over for a treat.

"There's my girl," Kaitlin murmured. Opening the door, she stepped inside, noting that someone had taken off Sterling's blanket. As she gave the mare a carrot, she found herself wishing that she could just skip riding altogether and go home. But there was no way. After her layup, Sterling needed to get out, if only for a hack.

While the mare chewed, she nudged Kaitlin's pockets. "That's all the carrots I brought," Kaitlin said. "Anyway, you haven't finished the one you're eating."

"Hi there."

Kaitlin's head snapped up at the sound of Connor's voice.

"What are you doing here?" she gasped, looking straight into his face.

Connor threw her a brilliant smile, and Kaitlin was

conscious that the interior of the barn suddenly seemed to light up, as if someone had flipped on all the light switches.

"I called your house, but your sister said you were here. So, well, here I am."

She opened the stall door a bit wider, gesturing Connor to come in.

"This is Sterling," Kaitlin said, her pride coming through in her voice.

"Hello, Sterling," Connor said, stepping into the stall and looking at the mare. He shoved his hands in his pockets and stood close to the wall. Sterling came over and flared her nostrils, taking in his scent suspiciously. "She's kinda big," he added.

"Not that big," Kaitlin replied. "She's a little over sixteen hands. You should see some of the other horses around here at Whisperwood. They're well over seventeen hands, and Tor's got a couple of warmbloods that are at least eighteen. Now that's big!"

"Yeah?" Connor glanced at Kaitlin, his eyes sweeping over her.

Kaitlin was embarrassed that he was looking so intently at her, but she had to admit she liked it. Just then Sterling swung her head toward Connor and snorted, showering him with bright orange carrot bits.

"Ugh," he yelped, jumping back against the wall.

"Sterling! Mind your manners," Kaitlin scolded her mare. "Sorry about that," she apologized to Connor.

Connor wiped his jacket and turned to give her a smile. "No biggie," he said quickly. Kaitlin felt her cheeks flame as she turned to check Sterling's waterer.

He came looking for me, she thought happily.

"Actually, I stopped by to see if we were still on for the barbecue," he said. "I'm sorry I didn't confirm it sooner, but I've been pretty busy. Do you still want to go?"

He remembered! Kaitlin beamed and was about to nod. Suddenly she swallowed hard and glanced at Sterling.

"I'd love to, but I—um—blew off my lesson yesterday, so I have to ride today," she said, disappointment filling her. "I just can't get out of it, or Sam—she's my instructor— she'll kill me. And Sterling . . . well, she just won't understand. You see, we're training for this horse trial, and—" Kaitlin was suddenly conscious that she was babbling, and she stopped abruptly.

"That's too bad," Connor said, shifting his weight and rocking on his heels.

He looks bummed, Kaitlin thought as Sterling tugged against the lead rope. She tossed her lovely head and pawed at the barn aisle. Kaitlin found herself wishing fiercely that she could just put her away and go with Connor. But Sterling needed to get out, and Kaitlin would not forgive herself for not doing what she knew was right.

Life is so unfair sometimes! she thought angrily. But then a sudden inspiration hit her.

"Want to go for a ride instead?" she asked, turning to Connor.

Connor appeared to consider it for a few seconds. "Me, ride? Sure, why not?" he replied slowly. "They'll just have to do without me at the barbecue."

"I'll borrow some boots for you and go ask Sam if we can use one of the school horses," exclaimed Kaitlin, the wheels turning in her head.

Connor's eyebrows shot up. "School horses?"

Suddenly Kaitlin realized that she'd probably insulted him. Since Connor was used to riding, he probably wouldn't appreciate being put on a poky old school horse.

"Wait, I know a better horse for you—Megaton," Kaitlin said.

Megaton was a retired jumper that belonged to one of Tor's clients. Though the gelding was nearing twenty years old, he still had plenty of energy.

"Megaton?" Connor repeated.

"You'll like him," she said, motioning Connor to wait.

Leading Sterling quickly down the barn aisle, Kaitlin caught up with Sam at the cross ties.

"Sam, can I borrow Megaton for my friend Connor to ride?" she asked eagerly. "He's ridden lots, and I know he could handle him."

She was conscious that Alicia and Madison, who were grooming school horses in the cross ties, were staring at her.

Sam hesitated for a second before nodding her head. "I don't think Tor would mind, as long as you don't push the old guy," she said. "His arthritis is acting up. He's got more *oomph* than is good for his joints at his age."

"We'll take care of him," Kaitlin said, scurrying away happily.

A few minutes later Kaitlin and Connor were mounted.

"Let's head over to the cross-country course so you can see it," she said, looking out the corner of her eye.

Connor sure looks amazing on a horse, she thought, taking in his long, lean frame and noting how tall he sat in his saddle. His light hair contrasted with Megaton's shiny black coat.

While Kaitlin swung Sterling's head around, she noticed the riding students making their way over to the outdoor arena. Madison and Alicia turned to look at her, and Kaitlin felt a teeny surge of triumph. *Check it out, ladies. I don't only think about horses,* she thought, tossing her head.

The morning sun rose higher in the sky as Kaitlin and Connor rode side by side up the hill. Kaitlin felt a warmth spread through her, one that wasn't entirely due to the sunshine.

Connor kept up a steady stream of conversation, and

84

Kaitlin found that she didn't have to say much. From time to time, she caught herself stealing glances at him, noting his handsome profile and correct hand position.

He hasn't ridden in a while, but he has quiet hands, she thought. "Where did you learn to ride?" she blurted out.

Connor shrugged. "At this little academy near where I used to live in Florida," he replied. He picked up Megaton's reins suddenly. "Want to race up the hill?" he asked.

Kaitlin felt her adrenaline surge for a few seconds, thinking how much Sterling would like to race. But she reluctantly shook her head. "Can't," she said. "I need to conserve her. We've got a cross-country lesson tomorrow."

"Too bad," Connor replied. "Well, then, is it okay if I take this horsepower up the hill by myself? He sure wants to go."

Kaitlin bit her lip before shaking her head. "Sorry," she mumbled. "Megaton's got some arthritis issues, and Sam says we have to take it easy on him, too."

"I'll take it easy. I'll just let him blow out his carburetor a little," Connor replied, leaning forward and getting ready to dig his heels into the old horse's sides.

"No, really, I'm not supposed to let him gallop." Kaitlin was alarmed. "Um, maybe some other time I can find you another horse. There are lots of fast ones around here."

"Oh," Connor said, disappointment spreading across his face.

"We can trot over here and cross the river by the lake, though, if you want," Kaitlin said hastily.

"Lead the way!" Connor exclaimed.

Kaitlin rushed forward, determined to make it seem as though they were able to do something at least halfway interesting instead of just poke along. Unfortunately, by the time they arrived at the lake, Megaton's rib cage was heaving, and he was blowing.

Kaitlin swallowed, looking at the old horse. But she knew what she had to do. "I think we'd better turn back."

Back at the barn, as they climbed off their horses, Connor smiled and said, "Thanks, that was fun."

Kaitlin didn't think he sounded too enthusiastic.

"Listen, I have to dash," Connor said once they'd clipped the horses in the cross ties. He grabbed Kaitlin's hand before walking to his car. "Let's do this again soon, okay?"

Kaitlin was so happy, she hardly minded that he'd left her to groom and clean up Megaton as well as her own horse.

"He probably had some important things to do," she told herself, picking up her grooming box.

Well, so do I, she thought with a little bitterness. Deep Woods was less than a week away.

7

THE NEXT FEW DAYS WERE A WHIRLWIND OF ACTIVITY AS KAITLIN stepped up her preparation for the trial. After he'd left her hanging on Sunday, she'd tried to force Connor out of her mind. Each day after school, she worked on an aspect of the trial—dressage, cross-country, and stadium jumping. Though she still leaned occasionally, Sam corrected her immediately and stayed steadfastly positive.

On Wednesday, Kaitlin sat in English class, doodling in her notebook while Mr. Thatcher droned on about literary devices. She had just drawn the cross-country course at Deep Woods and was studying direct and indirect routes when a note landed on her desk. Looking up, she saw that it came from Connor.

Can you come to the play rehearsal after school today? she read.

Sighing, she turned and shook her head. She was scheduled for a jumping session with Tor. Parker would be schooling with her on Ozzie since he too was preparing for the trial. Connor mouthed, "Why not?" Kaitlin was about to write back but decided not to risk passing a note. Instead, she pantomimed jumping a course with her fingers, using some pens set up around her desk as fences.

After class, Connor hurried out, and Kaitlin shook her head as she put on her heavy backpack.

She thought about Connor all through her jumping lesson, and afterward Parker flipped up her hair with his riding crop as he pulled up next to her on Ozzie. "You're lucky Tor's got twins on the brain since today's Sam's checkup," he whispered so Tor wouldn't hear. "Otherwise he'd chew you out for the way you zoned out here just now."

Kaitlin batted the crop away. "I didn't zone out," she protested. "We just didn't click today. And anyway, Parker Townsend, you didn't exactly have the best session yourself. Ozzie seemed more interested in jumping *out* of the arena than in jumping anything that happened to be *in* it."

Parker grinned. "That's Ozzie for you," he said philosophically.

The next day, Kaitlin found herself once again in the

position of having to turn Connor down when he asked her to go with him to the new coffeehouse in town.

"I can't!" she exclaimed. "I've got this horse trial I'm preparing for, and today I've got another lesson."

"Do you ride every day?" Connor asked.

"No," Kaitlin replied.

"Could have fooled me," Connor said.

Kaitlin tried to think of a reply but couldn't. She watched him disappear among the throng of students in the hallway, and felt a wave of despair.

"I don't know about this," she declared darkly on Friday afternoon. She and Parker were loading the trailer with the equipment they'd need for the first day of the trial. Deep Woods was only an hour away, so they'd return to Whisperwood in the evening and drive back the next morning for the next two phases. Parker was taking Ozzie to school, and four other Whisperwood students were going as well.

"Don't know about what?" Parker asked while he worked.

"I'm probably nuts to be competing, the way things have been going lately," replied Kaitlin.

"Quite honestly, I've seen you ride better, but there's still hope," Parker told her. "Just put your heart into it, and you'll do fine."

Kaitlin sighed. She couldn't help thinking that putting her heart into her riding was a big part of the problem. She picked up Sterling's worn cooler and placed it on top of the others.

"Have you been chewing on that thing as well as your nails?" Parker joked, glancing at the tattered cooler.

"No," Kaitlin replied, glaring and shoving her hands in her jeans pockets. "I guess I do need a new one, though."

Maybe, she decided impulsively, she'd bring along some money she'd saved and see if she could find a fancy show cooler at one of the tack concessions. Sterling would look magnificent parading around the grounds in it. The thought cheered her up momentarily.

"Okay. We've got the feed, supplements, buckets, chains, stall guards, and all the tack, right? I'll go get the first-aid kit," Parker said, whistling as he headed toward the barn.

Listening to Parker's happy whistle made Kaitlin's spirits sink right back down again. His excitement about competing was in direct contrast to the way she felt.

Just the thought of the grueling tests coming up made her feel tired beyond belief. She felt unbelievably resentful about all the work she'd put in so far. It didn't help that on top of everything, she'd had to turn down Connor twice when he'd asked her out. It wasn't like she was dying to sit through a play rehearsal or go somewhere to sip coffee, but she was still disappointed that they hadn't been able to hang out.

How am I ever going to get a relationship off the ground if I can never go out on a real date? she fumed. *All because of a trial that I'll probably completely bomb anyway.*

Sighing, Kaitlin walked over to the cross ties, looking for her grooming box so that she could load it into the trailer. She paused when she saw Allie crouched down next to Sterling, touching up the mare's fetlocks and straightening to trim Sterling's jawline with tiny manicure scissors.

What's she doing? Kaitlin wondered. *I just finished trimming Sterling.*

Of course, she remembered with a tinge of guilt, she had kind of rushed the job. Still, she wasn't thrilled that the younger girl was now going back over her work. Kaitlin was about to say something, but after examining Sterling's fetlocks, she closed her mouth. There was no doubt that Allie's steady hands had improved upon Kaitlin's trimming. Kaitlin knew she should be glad, but instead she found herself thinking about how Allie always seemed to be right on her heels. It was as though she was always trying to show Kaitlin how much better she was at everything.

All right, Allie, you win. Why don't you just take over Sterling while you're at it? Kaitlin thought irritably, leaning over to pick up her grooming box. Kaitlin was being unfair, and she knew it. But worrying about competing and wishing

91

she had time for Connor definitely weren't helping her mood.

"This ought to be everything, I think," Parker said as he approached holding the equine first-aid kit and some extra polo wraps.

"I'll go through the equipment one last time and mark everything off on the checklist," replied Kaitlin automatically.

"Attagirl," Parker said, ruffling her hair as he walked past her. "Where would we be without Ms. Organized?"

Kaitlin smiled in spite of herself, pleased at the compliment.

Just then Allie stood up. "I hope you don't mind my helping," she said quietly, tucking the scissors into her pocket.

"Not at all," Kaitlin replied, feeling embarrassed that Allie had detected her annoyance.

"It's just that I know Sterling is a little ticklish, and it makes it hard to trim her without having some raggedy edges," Allie added.

Kaitlin tried to keep her expression neutral, but Allie's possessive tone made her want to scream. "True," she mumbled evenly.

"Look," Allie added after a slight pause. "I know you've been leasing Sterling forever, but if for any reason you ever, um, get too busy for her, could you let me know first?"

Allie's words were like a slap in the face to Kaitlin. What in the world did Allie mean by that?

"Don't worry," she snapped. "I'll never be too busy for Sterling."

With that, Kaitlin marched down the barn aisle and ducked into the tack room, fighting the urge to kick something.

8

"KAITLIN, I CAN'T FIND SCOOTER'S GIRTH," YELLED MORGAN shrilly.

"Well, then look again," Kaitlin replied. She was busy digging through her garment bag for her hairnet. It was Saturday morning, and she and Parker and several students had pulled into the parking lot at Deep Woods for the trial. Since Sam wouldn't arrive till later, Kaitlin had helped get some of the beginners tacked up for their dressage tests. She'd figured Morgan could saddle himself up, so she could get ready for her own upcoming test.

"I've looked three times, and there's no girth anywhere," Morgan persisted. He planted himself in front of Kaitlin and glared.

He looks just like an angry little penguin, Kaitlin thought, glancing at his dressage habit.

"Well, come on," Morgan whined. "You've got to find it!"

"Say please," Kaitlin replied, struggling to maintain a light tone so that Morgan wouldn't get himself really worked up. "I'm not your personal valet."

She started digging through the pile of tack she and Parker had packed in the truck the day before. Scooter's girth was nowhere to be found.

"How can that be?" she muttered, anxiety creeping into her voice. "I know it's around here somewhere."

Suddenly Kaitlin got a mental flash of the girth hanging from the cleaning hook outside the tack room. *It's still there*, she realized. *I didn't go over the checklist!* She'd been too busy stewing about Allie instead.

"Omigosh. I think I forgot the girth," she whispered, slapping her forehead.

"You forgot it? Now what are we going to do?" Morgan said, panicked. "I'll have to scratch, and my mom and dad will have to forfeit the fees, and—"

Kaitlin held up her hand and shushed him. She pressed her fingers to her temples and closed her eyes.

"Let me think," she said. Though she sounded calm, inside her brain was whirling. She could just imagine what would happen if Morgan wasn't able to ride that day because he didn't have a girth. She had to find a replacement right away. But how? It wasn't as though she had all the time in the world to wander the grounds and look for one to borrow. Morgan was riding in mere minutes. And even if she did find one that someone wasn't using, it probably wouldn't fit. Scooter had a huge barrel and needed a larger-than-average girth.

I'm in trouble, Kaitlin thought, ripping at a fingernail. *Sam won't ever trust me again!*

Gazing across the parking lot, she suddenly saw a row of concession stands set up next to the show office, and a lightbulb went off in her head. She patted her pocket with the money she'd brought for Sterling's fancy new cooler and felt a sharp pang. She would have to use the money to buy Morgan a new girth instead.

Well, it's your fault, she chided herself.

"Wait right here," she barked at Morgan. She waved frantically at Parker, who was busy giving Penny and Justin a leg up. "I'll be right back," she called out to him, darting over to the stands.

Coffee, hot dogs, breakfast foods, equine antiques and gifts . . . Kaitlin read each sign as she ran along in front of the booths. Finally, at the end, she found what she was looking for: *Molly's Horse Parlor. Tack and Equipment for the Discerning Rider.*

Kaitlin gulped as she reached into her pocket for her money. She knew what "discerning rider" meant, all right:

expensive. Even if she was lucky enough to find a girth to fit Scooter's generous dimensions, she would pay through the nose for her mistake. *Good-bye, new cooler,* she thought bleakly.

Sighing with relief, Kaitlin located the girth she needed. It was hidden, hanging on a rack behind some martingales. Hurriedly she snatched it off the rack.

"How much?" she asked the bored wanna-be rocker working behind the card table.

The worker looked at her with half-closed eyes and shrugged. "I'll check." But he made no move to do anything.

"Please," Kaitlin pleaded, "I'm in a hurry. The kid who needs this rides his test in just a few minutes."

The guy appeared to be unimpressed. "That's a specialty item, you know," he drawled.

Kaitlin nodded.

"Hard to find girths that big," he added.

"Yes, I know," Kaitlin said between clenched teeth. She wanted to scream.

The worker finally named a price that made Kaitlin gasp.

"That much?" she squeaked. "The tack shops in Lexington don't charge half that!"

The wanna-be rocker smiled wickedly. "The nearest tack shop will be almost an hour, round trip. And it might not carry this girth that you're in such a hurry to have. Take it or leave it," he added.

Kaitlin knew she had no choice. Reluctantly she slapped the money on the table and dashed out of the booth. She had no time to haggle with anyone. Morgan was supposed to be warming up already. She'd just have to suck it up and vow not to be so forgetful next time.

If there is a next time, she growled inside, feeling as though she never wanted to go to another event as long as she lived. She dashed back to help Morgan tack up. The girth was new and stiff, and it seemed to take forever to buckle.

"I'm going to be late," Morgan whined.

When Morgan was finally mounted and riding toward the schooling ring, Kaitlin wiped her brow. Finally she could turn back to her own preparation.

By the time Kaitlin was dressed in her dark dressage habit and mounted on Sterling, she was a jittery mess. She tugged at her stock, which wasn't tied as perfectly as she'd have wanted it, before picking up her reins. On her way over to the schooling ring she realized she didn't have her number. Frantically she turned Sterling around and hurried back to the trailer.

"Where's my number?" she wailed to Parker.

Parker frowned and held it up. "Right here," he said as he pinned it on her back. "Talk about role reversal. Usually you're the one who saves my bacon. This time I'm the organized knight in shining armor."

"All hail the magnificent knight," Kaitlin said breathlessly. "I owe you one. Thanks."

She started over to the schooling ring and had just started her warm-up when she felt her hair flop against her neck. Reaching up, she realized her hairnet had fallen off, and the bun she'd crafted quickly had come undone.

"Boyce, you're a certified mess," she muttered, frantically trying to stuff her hair back in place while holding Sterling's reins with one hand.

Sam would kill me if she could see my turnout, Kaitlin thought when she was finally able to start schooling.

She was only halfway warmed up when the announcer's voice crackled over the PA system.

"Number ninety-nine, on deck."

"That's me," Kaitlin yelped.

As she walked around the outside of the arena and waited for the competitor before her to finish, she felt her hands shaking. Her stomach started flip-flopping when she saw how impressive the rider before her was. When she entered the arena, she could tell that Sterling had absorbed her nervousness. She didn't halt squarely for the salute at X. And instead of the working trot the test called for, Sterling jigged for the first two steps.

That'll cost us, Kaitlin thought fleetingly.

Summoning all her willpower, Kaitlin forced herself to breathe deeply and steadied Sterling. At first the pace was slightly uneven, but Sterling quickly responded to Kaitlin's quieter hands. By the time they were tracking left, Kaitlin had Sterling perfectly framed. At H, it was time to lengthen the stride for a rising trot.

When it was time to change rein at M, Kaitlin cued Sterling smoothly. At the exact moment she asked for the working trot, Sterling moved out with form and precision.

Now we're cooking, Kaitlin thought, feeling the timeless magic of a horse and rider in perfect sync. She and Sterling went through the next series of transitions perfectly. She only caught herself leaning one time. *Balance, balance*, she repeated to herself.

After picking up the working canter at F, Kaitlin and Sterling executed a correct change of lead.

That was poetry in motion! Kaitlin exulted. She and Sterling performed the rest of the test flawlessly, and Kaitlin was almost giddy as she and Sterling went up the centerline. There they stopped, and Kaitlin saluted the judges.

As she started trotting out of the arena, Kaitlin was startled to see Connor standing next to Parker.

What's he doing here? Kaitlin thought. Forgetting that she was still being judged until she was completely out of the arena, she transferred her reins to one gloved hand and waved. Immediately she caught Parker's frantic signal, and she lowered her hand sheepishly.

I can't believe I did that, Kaitlin thought. *I wonder how many penalty points that'll cost me.*

But as she approached Connor, she shrugged. It didn't matter. What mattered was that Connor was there.

"Hi, Connor!" she exclaimed, purposely avoiding Parker's glance. "You took me completely off guard. I was so surprised to see you."

Connor pretended to be hurt. He tried to look sorrowful, but his eyes sparkled. "Sorry I came?"

"No, no," Kaitlin said hastily, dismounting and loosening Sterling's girth. "That's a good thing."

"Great." Connor grinned broadly, and he gingerly reached over to pat Sterling's damp shoulder. "Parker here tells me he's your instructor."

Kaitlin nodded. "He is. So tell me, did you see my whole test? What did you think?"

The question was directed at Connor, but Parker answered.

"Kind of a bobbly start, don't you think?" Parker replied, moving directly in front of Connor to place a rug on Sterling's hindquarters. As he did so, he locked eyes with Kaitlin. "Never mind the grand finale."

"Well, everything in between went pretty well. That's enough for me," Kaitlin snapped, and she looked past him toward Connor. "So are you going to stay for a while?" she asked him.

"It was obvious that you didn't warm up enough,"

Parker went on, stepping over so that he once again blocked her view of Connor.

Kaitlin frowned. She knew Parker was right, but did he have to be a jerk and analyze her shortcomings right in front of Connor? Fuming, she pulled her reins over Sterling's head and started walking her in a small circle.

Connor wiped Sterling's sweat on his jeans. "Don't worry, Kaitlin," he said quietly. "*I* didn't see anything wrong. *I* thought you did fine."

"Thanks," Kaitlin said. Glaring at Parker, she added, "At least *someone* thinks so."

"What did you think of Sterling's pace after the salute at X?" Parker asked Connor in a tone of voice that Kaitlin couldn't quite decipher. "And just how many penalty points do you think Kaitlin racked up at the end when she totally fell apart and waved before she had made her exit?"

Connor shifted his weight from foot to foot. "Beats me," he said. "I know nothing about dressade, or whatever you call it."

"Dressage," Kaitlin said quickly. "It's just the French word for 'training.'"

She shot daggers at Parker, furious that he'd asked the questions just to embarrass Connor.

"Wow, do I feel stupid," Connor replied with a forced laugh.

"Oh, don't mind Parker," Kaitlin said, stopping Sterling

and slipping her arm through Connor's. "He thinks that because I don't have any big brothers to annoy me, he needs to step in and fill the role."

"Amazing," Parker said dryly. "One minute I'm a knight in shining armor, and the next I'm just an annoying big brother trying to keep a certain someone from making a fool of herself and Sterling."

"'He doth nothing but talk of his horse,'" Connor quoted.

Parker darted a questioning glance at him.

"It's a quotation. Connor knows I like them," Kaitlin explained quickly. "Shakespeare again?"

Connor smiled approvingly. "From *The Merchant of Venice*."

"Shakespeare? What's he got to do with dressage?" Parker muttered, looking disgusted.

"Should I leave? Do you two need to talk alone?" Connor asked, suddenly looking incredibly uncomfortable.

"No!" Kaitlin replied. "We're done."

Connor smiled. "Well, then, let's get outta here. To tell you the truth, dressage bores the heck out of me."

Kaitlin's eyes flicked involuntarily over to Parker's face. "It kind of bores me too at times," she said, trying to smooth things over. "I totally prefer cross-country."

"I'll go get Ozzie tacked up," Parker said, turning abruptly on his heel. "Maybe after you've cooled Sterling,

Kaitlin, we can go over a few more *boring* little dressage fine points. That is, if you actually remember to *cool* the horse that just gave you her all out there in that *boring* dressage arena."

Kaitlin felt her cheeks flame.

Connor jerked his chin in Parker's direction and raised an eyebrow. "Is your instructor always that touchy?" he asked.

Instantly Kaitlin felt protective of Parker, even though she wanted to kick him for being so rude. "Oh, he's all right," she said quickly. "It's just that he's got a lot on his mind. You see, he always gets a little worked up when he's competing, and he's got this difficult horse to ride, and—"

She stopped when she realized Connor wasn't listening. He was looking at her in amusement. "No more horse talk," he said, putting his finger to her lips. "Let's blow this place and go do something. Have you had lunch yet? Maybe we could go for a swim."

"A swim?" Kaitlin's head was spinning. "Isn't it awfully cold?"

"My parents just installed an indoor pool," Connor said. "It's heated."

A heated pool—wouldn't that feel nice on her sore muscles! Kaitlin was about to nod when suddenly she glanced at Sterling, who was dark with sweat, and her heart thudded to her boots. "Can't," she said. "I've got to cool Sterling and give her a bath and rubdown."

"That shouldn't take all afternoon," Connor replied.

"Well, the truth is, I can't go out at all," Kaitlin said. "This is only day one of the trial, and I've got lots of other stuff to do to get ready for tomorrow. I'm helping with the lesson students, and after the tests are over, we have to pack up the horses and equipment and head back to Whisperwood."

"Okay, so we skip the swim. I'll pick you up tonight after you get back, and we'll go to dinner and a movie," Connor persisted.

Kaitlin took off her cap and ran her hand through her wet hair. "I just can't. I've got to go to bed early. I'm riding the cross-country and stadium jumping phases tomorrow, and I've got an early draw."

Connor nodded, but he looked bewildered. "Let me get this straight," he said slowly. "You have to go bed early on a Saturday night just so that the next day you can sit there while your horse plops over a few logs? I mean, the horse is doing all the work. You just go along for the ride and do nothing."

Kaitlin was puzzled. Where had she ever gotten the idea that he understood anything about eventing? It was becoming crystal clear that he didn't know the first thing about it. Though Connor had said he didn't want to talk horses, she couldn't resist trying to explain it to him. Maybe he'd understand better where she was coming from.

"Cross-country's a little more than just plopping over a few logs," she replied. "It's the heart of the whole sport of eventing, and I've had to prepare for it for months. I'm riding in the preliminary division, and some of the fences are three foot seven. And we have to finish a course of about twenty-one jumps within a strict time frame, or we get time penalties. Once that's over, we jump in an arena. That's called stadium jumping."

Connor nodded. "Sounds exciting."

"It definitely is!" Kaitlin exclaimed, aware that she was babbling and that she sounded like a textbook. Hurriedly, she added, "You ought to come out here tomorrow and see my go, if you have time. It's nothing like dressage."

"Yeah, maybe I'll see if I can," Connor said evenly. "Well, it was nice watching you ride. See ya around."

"See ya," Kaitlin echoed. Hot tears pricked at the back of her eyes as she watched him walk away. It was obvious he still didn't understand what all the fuss was about. She felt her heart thud into her polished boots when she saw him pull out his cell phone as he disappeared into the crowd.

9

"YOU OKAY, KAITLIN?" CHRISTINA ASKED AS THE WHISPERWOOD trailer rolled into the parking lot at Deep Woods just after first light on Sunday morning. Parker was driving, Christina beside him. Kaitlin, who was sitting by the door, felt her mouth go dry.

"Just my usual pre-event nerve spiral," she tried to joke.

She was always nervous before the cross-country phase. But that day was worse than ever because she knew she'd have to do extra well if she wanted to make up for the previous day's dressage penalties. It didn't help that she'd stayed up half the night thinking about Connor and wondering who he'd found to keep him company since she hadn't been able to.

Now Kaitlin glanced at Parker's profile and felt anger mix with her nerves. It was a good thing Christina had decided at the last minute to come along, partly because that meant Kaitlin didn't have to talk to Parker—at least till they walked the cross-country course. She was still furious at how he'd baited Connor after her dressage test.

A few minutes later, however, Kaitlin softened toward Parker when she saw the caring way he helped Christina out of the truck and handed her her crutches.

"Make yourself comfortable," Parker said, tenderly leading Christina over to a portable chair he'd set up for her. "After we unload, I'll run and get you a bagel and some hot cocoa, okay?"

"Stupid leg of mine. I feel so useless just sitting here. I wish I could help," Christina said with a catch in her voice.

Parker touched her cheek. "You *are* helping just by being here," he said cheerfully. "And don't worry. We'll put you to work keeping track of everyone's times."

Okay, so you're not a total jerk, Kaitlin thought grudgingly as she watched him kiss Christina lightly.

She was suddenly horrified to find herself wondering what it would be like to be kissed by Connor. *Like that'll happen after the way everything went down yesterday*, she thought sarcastically. She made a horrible face as she went around to the back of the rig to lower the ramp for the horses. *You'll be lucky if he ever speaks to you again*, Kaitlin thought, glancing

108

at the gunmetal-gray sky and shivering in her fleece jacket. She frowned and tried to direct her thoughts back to getting ready for the next two phases of the trial.

Luckily, that morning went more smoothly than the day before had. Kaitlin was able to walk the cross-country course in plenty of time. She and Parker stuck to talking about the technicalities of the course, so they didn't risk adding anything to the tension that existed between them.

Kaitlin also managed to get Penny, Justin, and Morgan tacked up and mounted without incident. She watched them ride toward the schooling area with Parker just before she ducked into the small compartment at the front of the trailer to change. Yanking off her fleece, she put on her protective vest and number pinny over her shirt. Then she pulled on her armband with her medical information on it. Finally she grabbed her helmet and stopwatch and went to get Sterling.

After she put on the gray mare's protective boots and tacked her up, Kaitlin climbed aboard. She took Sterling over to the crowded warm-up arena. While she was trotting, she looked over in time to see Parker walk up to the schooling arena and lean against the rail to watch her.

"Plenty of warm-up today," he said crisply. "Not like yesterday."

I knew he'd get a dig in, Kaitlin thought irritably. *I wish he'd go take care of Ozzie and leave me alone.*

"You want warm-up? Watch this," she muttered under

her breath. She continued trotting, then cued Sterling into a rocking canter and went around the ring a few times before reversing. She popped Sterling over several schooling fences that were set up in the center of the arena.

"That enough?" she called out testily.

"You tell me," came Parker's maddening answer.

Kaitlin stuffed down her annoyance and took Sterling over a few more fences. Finally Parker gave her a thumbs-up and motioned her over to the rail.

Kaitlin was tempted to ride past Parker and go straight to the starting box. But she thought better of it and rode over to get her last-minute instructions. She might be mad at Parker, but she knew she'd be foolish to ignore his advice at this critical time.

"All right," Parker said, checking the studs in Sterling's back shoes as the steward called Kaitlin's number. "Be smart out there. Pay attention. Don't take too many chances, but if Sterling's going well, don't be afraid to be a little aggressive."

Kaitlin, who was suddenly so nervous that she wanted to throw up, simply nodded. All her anger at Parker dissolved as she looked at him for reassurance.

"There's a good rider in you, Triple Threat," he said suddenly, giving her a crooked grin. "Just let her come out to play."

Kaitlin smiled back and gave him a cheery salute, then

made her way to the starting box, her heart pounding.

"Ten, nine, eight, seven . . ."

Kaitlin's head throbbed as she sat in the starting box, Sterling's hindquarters facing the opening. Sterling was coiled like a spring, waiting to explode from the box the second the official said, "Go!"

When the moment came, Sterling whirled around and shot out of the box just as Kaitlin set her stopwatch. They were off! While they thundered toward their first fence, Kaitlin felt the cold wind slapping at her face. Soon tears were streaming from her eyes. Blinking rapidly, she mentally kicked herself for forgetting her goggles. But there was no time to worry about it. Hurriedly she lowered herself into a forward position on the approach to the large, imposing log pile jump.

Sterling rocked back and took off with a mighty effort, landing perfectly on the other side.

One down, Kaitlin thought, her blood coursing through her. *Twenty more to go.*

With that, she cued Sterling up the hill, and they made their way along the galloping track toward the next fence, a ditch with a bending line, followed by a second element.

Sterling negotiated the next few jumps with boldness and accuracy, and Kaitlin began to relax just a little. Out of the corner of her eye, she could see spectators lining the edge of the course.

Was Connor among them? The unbidden thought came into her mind, temporarily distracting her. Kaitlin's hands closed abruptly on her reins, and Sterling must have felt it—she threw in a little buck of protest at being held back.

"Sorry, girl," Kaitlin mumbled as they tore across the course.

She frowned in concentration when they neared the next fence, which was a tricky upright.

Sterling took it perfectly and afterward tossed her head, begging to be allowed to go faster.

"Save your energy, silly," Kaitlin murmured lovingly to her mare. "We need to finish this course, and that nasty big bank is still up ahead."

She knew she shouldn't think of anything but her next fence, but she found herself trying to scan the crowd, unconsciously slowing Sterling as she did so.

The mare fought against Kaitlin's uncharacteristic hold and galloped on in a zigzag pattern. Suddenly they were in front of the bank.

Bad approach, Kaitlin thought frantically. She tried to correct the mare, but Sterling took the jump much too slowly, landing awkwardly and having to scramble to make it down the other side without toppling forward.

Whew, that was close. Kaitlin forced herself to stop checking out the spectators lined up alongside the course. Fleetingly she wondered what Connor would think if he could see her ride.

Pay attention, Triple Threat. Parker's words echoed in her head.

Partway through the course, Kaitlin checked her watch and realized that they were somewhat behind. She was on her way to collecting needless penalties. It was time to kick it up a notch.

"Let's rock, Sterling," she called out, crouching low on Sterling's neck and kneading her fingers through Sterling's mane.

Sterling responded by lengthening her stride and throwing in another little buck as if to say, *Finally!* Kaitlin wanted to let out a whoop of pure pleasure.

This is probably how Christina feels when she's racing, Kaitlin thought, momentarily filled with extra adrenaline. Suddenly, however, she pictured Christina as she'd left her only an hour ago—sitting by the trailer next to her crutches and wistfully watching everyone else ride.

Christina's not racing anymore, Kaitlin reminded herself. *And she might not ever be able to get on a horse again. She's got to sit there while other people race Star, and there's not a thing she can do about it.*

"Horses, heartbreak," she remembered hearing an old horseman once saying. *Isn't that the truth,* she thought sourly, remembering the way Connor had looked the previous day when she'd told him she couldn't go out because she had to stay with the horses.

"Stop it," Kaitlin said aloud, realizing her thoughts had

once again strayed off course. For a split second she panicked when she realized she had no idea where the next fence was. *That's what you get for thinking about other things,* she scolded herself. Luckily, as she and Sterling flew up the hill, she remembered that the bounce was the next obstacle, followed by a tricky hedge. She checked the flags for extra reassurance, and she and Sterling negotiated the bounce.

Kaitlin stood in her irons while Sterling swept up the grassy track toward the water jump. As they approached, Kaitlin noted the particularly large crowd of spectators gathered nearby.

She balanced Sterling carefully in front of the first element, a huge log, closing her legs and giving her just enough rein to make the mighty effort up over the obstacle and into the water.

"Three-two-one," Kaitlin counted after Sterling splashed down, sending up a spray as she collected herself to spring out. After successfully negotiating the step out, she was surprised to find that she didn't feel her usual elation.

Focus, she thought.

The pair continued through the course until finally they were shooting toward the last obstacle. By now Kaitlin's face burned from the cold wind, and her legs felt like rubber. But she never took her eyes off the jump ahead, positioning Sterling carefully. When they landed on the other side, Kaitlin felt herself exhale. Seconds later they passed through the finish flags. They'd completed the course!

Kaitlin glanced at her stopwatch. They were several seconds over. *Time penalties*, Kaitlin thought with dismay. She'd never gotten time penalties before. Shaking her head, she began slowing Sterling.

"Sorry, girl," she mumbled, patting the mare's foam-flecked neck. "You were trying to tell me to pick up the pace. I guess I just wasn't listening."

She had just jumped off when Sam hurried over to her with a towel.

"How did it go?" Sam asked as she started rubbing Sterling vigorously.

"All right, I guess," panted Kaitlin. She scrambled to loosen Sterling's girth and check her respiration and heart-beat. Satisfied with the reading, she started to walk her. While she walked she found herself craning her neck to see if she could spot Connor anywhere in the crowd.

"I'm so sorry that I missed your go," Sam said, walking along beside her. "I just got here."

"Huh?" Kaitlin asked, peering over her head.

"I slept right through my alarm clock," Sam went on. "I couldn't believe it. The twins aren't even born yet, and already they're throwing off my schedule!"

Kaitlin didn't answer.

"So, tell me about your go," Sam said after a pause.

Kaitlin shrugged.

"I could use a little more detail here," Sam persisted.

"What jump were you stationed at?" Kaitlin asked.

Sam looked at her, puzzled. "I told you I just got here."

Kaitlin nodded quickly. "Oh, yeah, that's right. I got some time penalties, but other than that, it was okay."

Sam flung the wet towel over her shoulder and rubbed her lower back. "You're not one for time penalties. You must have chosen to go the conservative route," she said. "Any special reason?"

"No," Kaitlin replied. There was no way she wanted to confess to Sam that she'd been daydreaming over the course and had lost precious seconds. "I don't know what happened. I was just slow, that's all."

Sam considered that for a few seconds. Finally she said, "When you're finished walking Sterling, bring her back to the trailer, and we'll go over the stadium jumping course."

Suddenly Kaitlin spotted a guy with blond hair in the crowd by the parking lot, and her heart gave a leap. But when the guy turned around, she saw that it wasn't Connor.

"Rats," she said under her breath.

"Kaitlin, did you hear what I said?" Sam asked.

Kaitlin blinked. "Sorry," she mumbled. "Could you repeat that?"

Sam frowned disapprovingly and repeated herself. Then she added, "I hope you're back in the game by the time you enter the ring. I've seen the course, and believe me, it's no slam-dunk."

But Kaitlin didn't hear her. She was still scanning the crowd hopefully.

"I'm about ready to give up here!" Sam said, shaking her head and stalking off.

10

THAT EVENING KAITLIN STOMPED INTO HER BEDROOM AND THREW down her saddle and the garment bags containing her dirty show clothes. She was sweaty, exhausted, and sporting a swollen cheek and giant bruise under her eye from her fall over the brick wall. Her ears were still ringing from the talking-to Sam had given her for not paying attention around the stadium course. She knew she deserved it, but it didn't make her feel any better.

Please let Connor have e-mailed me, she thought, flicking on her computer. If she could just have one little sign that she hadn't scared him off for good, maybe it wouldn't sting so much to think about how badly she'd messed up at the trial.

But Kaitlin's mailbox was empty. She flung her mud-covered breeches and shirt savagely into the hamper and jumped into the shower, closing her eyes and wishing the water could wash away her disappointment. Afterward she flopped on her bed in her T-shirt and pajama bottoms, staring at the wall where her poster had been.

"Let me see your trophy," yelled Jordan as she burst into the room.

"I didn't get a trophy," Kaitlin grumbled, glancing at her little sister.

"Why not?" Jordan asked. "Did someone steal it from you?"

Kaitlin shrugged. "No," she replied. "According to Parker, I gave it away with both hands."

"Why would you give it away?" Jordan persisted. "Parker told us at your jumper show that you never met a trophy you didn't like."

"Listen, I don't want to talk about this anymore, okay?" Kaitlin said.

She was grateful when her mom called Jordan to help her set the table for dinner. She wanted to be alone and wallow in her misery without having to pretend it wasn't a huge deal.

For a few minutes Kaitlin replayed her rotten ride around the stadium course, but she stopped when she realized that it only made her even more depressed.

If only Connor had come or called or something, she thought. Then none of the other stuff would matter. Glaring at the silent phone, Kaitlin tossed a horsehead pillow at it.

This is stupid, she decided suddenly. *I always wait for him to get in touch with me. There's nothing wrong with me calling him.* She had no doubt that girls like Madison called guys all the time and never gave it a second thought.

Still, the idea of doing something so un-Kaitlin-like made her dizzy, and her hands shook as she punched in the number for information. Luckily, Connor's phone number was listed.

To Kaitlin's annoyance, no one answered. After the fourth ring, the answering machine started grinding out its message. For a split second she considered hanging up, but then she thought better of it.

"Hi, Connor. This is Kaitlin," she said into the phone. "Call me back when you can."

She was grateful that her family didn't ask too many questions about the trial during dinner. Apart from explaining how she'd banged up her cheekbone at the brick wall, Kaitlin didn't offer any details. Her mother, Kaitlin could tell, wanted to know more, but she didn't comment when Kaitlin changed the subject.

After dinner, Kaitlin reluctantly joined Lindy and Jordan in a board game. The entire time, however, she listened for the phone.

"You're not paying attention," Lindy said accusingly after a while, flipping the board so that all the pieces rolled onto the living room rug.

"Sorry," Kaitlin said. "I'm totally wiped out."

"You're always wiped. You're always cranky. You're just no fun anymore," Jordan complained.

"Let Kaitlin be," said Mrs. Boyce, coming into the room. "She's had a hard day."

You don't know the half of it, Kaitlin thought, excusing herself to go to her room. There she sat staring at her computer, willing Connor to instant-message her.

She had just fallen asleep when she heard the ping she'd been waiting for.

Eagerly she sprang out of bed.

"He is pure air and fire . . . he is indeed a horse," she read.

One of Connor's pop quizzes! Kaitlin thought, her heart leaping.

Probably Shakespeare, if I know you. But I don't know which play it's from, she typed.

It's from Henry V. *I got your phone message, but it was too late to call you back,* she read a few seconds later.

That's okay, she typed, jazzed to hear from Connor at last.

I was at this great film festival all day with my friends, Connor responded. *Too bad you had to miss it. It was a total blast!*

Kaitlin bit her lip as she read what he wrote about the

121

things he had seen and done that day. She didn't know anything about film, but suddenly she wished she'd gone. No matter what it was like, it had to have been more fun than Deep Woods. Looking over at her dresser mirror, she caught a glimpse of her swollen cheekbone and purplish black eye.

When she glanced back at her computer, she saw that Connor had written, *What did you do?*

What did I do? Kaitlin thought, wrinkling her nose, then wincing in pain. *Looked around at Deep Woods for you, like a lovesick puppy,* she thought. *Got lectured for not paying attention. Ate some mud at the brick wall. Got a black eye.* But she wrote, *Not much. Just plopped over some logs on my horse.*

Why am I not surprised? Connor typed back. *I think it's time that you, Kaitlin Boyce, wake up and realize that you need to get a life!*

The words seemed to dance across the screen, taunting her. Her first reaction was to be insulted. After all, she had a life—a life with Sterling and her eventing friends at Whisperwood. She had big goals that required big sacrifices, and she'd always been glad to make them. But as she considered that life, she began to feel more tired than she'd ever felt before. She was tired of being dirty and feeling itchy because she was covered with hay. She was tired of worrying about missing lessons, tired of making equipment checklists, tired of worrying about whether she was ducking fences, and tired of feeling nervous before competition. She was tired of Parker lecturing her while pretending he was joking, and tired of Sam always pushing her to do her best.

She was tired of horses.

The thought made her sit bolt upright, and for a few seconds she held her fingers poised above the keyboard as she struggled with the enormousness of it.

You're absolutely right, Connor, she finally typed. *I have no life, but that's about to change, big time!*

After signing off her computer, Kaitlin sat on her floor, watching the moon rise over the treetops. She felt strangely excited now, and her heart beat rapidly. She found herself looking around her room. She hadn't done a thing to it since she'd moved to Lexington. Everything about it screamed, *Crazy horse girl lives here!*

In the darkness, she could make out the outlines of her saddle hanging over her chair. Her model horse collection lined her shelves. Though she couldn't see the titles in the dark, she knew that every other book on her bookshelves was a horse book. Her walls were festooned with the ribbons she'd won over the years, and her dresser was covered with trophies and statuettes.

It was time to redecorate!

Kaitlin raced around her bedroom, fueled by nervous energy. She snatched and grabbed riding clothes, pillows, equipment, knickknacks, mementos, pictures. Anything that was horse-related got shoved into her closet. For almost an hour she worked, until the pile grew high. As a final touch, she topped the pile with the wadded-up eventing poster she'd meant to throw in the wastebasket days before.

When Kaitlin was finished, she slammed her door. Then she surveyed her almost bare room.

"There," she said quietly. "Much better."

When she got around to it, she'd stuff everything into bags, she decided. Then she'd drive it straight over to the charity drop-off. She'd be rid of it, and her closet would be practically empty.

Then I'll go shopping like normal girls do—at the mall instead of at the tack shop, she told herself firmly.

Grabbing a sheet of paper, she turned on her reading light and started making a shopping list. This list wasn't like the others she'd made through the years. It didn't include bits, bridles, equine first-aid kits, or breeches and helmets. Instead, it detailed things she'd need for the new Kaitlin, things such as a haircut, makeup, and nail polish—and clothes that didn't belong at a barn!

11

ON MONDAY, KAITLIN DROVE IN THE MIST TOWARD WHISPER-
wood on her way to school. It was her custom to look in on
Sterling first thing the day after a horse show or trial. Even
though the mare was unfailingly sound after a competition, Kaitlin always felt better after she'd double-checked
and made sure. But that morning, when she came around
the bend and saw Whisperwood's familiar wooden sign
suspended on its two white chains, something caused her
to hesitate. It was the realization that the new Kaitlin
absolutely did not want to set foot in a stable yard this
morning.

"Sterling will be fine. She really doesn't need me bugging her," the new Kaitlin muttered aloud.

You really ought to go take a look just to be sure, the old Kaitlin shot back.

Kaitlin swallowed hard, staging a mighty battle within herself. Her hands were ready to turn the wheel and steer the car into the driveway. Suddenly she locked her elbows and drove right past the barn.

Did I really just do that? Kaitlin was shocked at herself. She took her foot off the gas to slow just a little. Maybe, she decided, she ought to turn around.

No, she thought fiercely the next second, putting her foot back on the accelerator. *This is the new and improved Kaitlin, remember?*

All the way to school, she tried not to think about what she'd just done. Once she arrived at Henry Clay, it was easy to forget about everything but books, lockers, and fellow students. Especially one fellow student.

Connor was standing by the door of the attendance office when Kaitlin walked by. As she looked at his face, she felt her hands grow clammy. How would he react when he saw her? She was glad that she'd spent extra time getting dressed that morning. She didn't have her new haircut yet, or new clothes. But she was wearing a dark skirt that she'd always liked, as well as a cute top. And instead of her usual boring ponytail, she'd fluffed her hair when she'd dried it so that it framed her face softly. She'd applied some cover-up to her bruised cheekbone so that it didn't stand out so much.

126

"Hi," she said, tilting her head the way that she'd seen Madison do a time or two.

Connor smiled evenly. "You look different today," he said.

"I do?" Kaitlin was thrilled, and she couldn't resist preening just a little. Suddenly she realized that he was probably talking about her bruised cheekbone. Her hand flew up to her face. "Oh, you mean this," she mumbled.

"No," Connor protested, though he looked at it closely. "But now that you mention it, what happened?"

"Riding accident," she said simply.

Connor nodded knowingly.

Oh, great, Kaitlin thought. *Here I go again. He's probably convinced that I eat, sleep, and breathe horses.*

Hurriedly she asked him about how the school play was going, just to change the subject.

"Pretty well," Connor replied. "We've got the second act down. Now we're working on the third."

"What play is it, anyway?" Kaitlin asked, embarrassed that she hadn't thought about asking before.

"It's a spoof on Shakespeare's life written by a Henry Clay alum," Connor replied. "It's made up of selections from a bunch of his plays. Pretty funny stuff."

Kaitlin nodded and asked him a few more questions about it, and Connor seemed eager to fill her in. When the bell rang, he offered to walk her to class, still describing his role and some of the scenes. Kaitlin beamed as she fell in beside him. It was amazing, she thought. All she'd done was make up her mind to ditch the old Kaitlin, and already her life was looking much rosier. *I should have done this a long time ago.*

Throughout the morning, things continued going her way. She counted at least three compliments on her outfit. A few of Connor's friends stopped and talked with her in the hallway, and Kaitlin felt encouraged—it looked as if they were starting to accept her as one of the group.

During lunch, however, Michaela set her brown bag down on the table next to her and looked at her in a way that made her realize something wasn't right.

"Listen, I know it's not my business," Michaela said, "but Connor is my friend. He really likes you, but he told me you confuse him."

"I do?" Kaitlin was surprised.

Michaela nodded. "He says you always seem glad to see him, but he's beginning to think that you're just making excuses not to go out with him," she said, giving Kaitlin a searching glance. "But I told him that you weren't. I'm right, aren't I?"

Kaitlin nodded quickly. "I didn't mean for him to think I was making excuses," she said. "I was just incredibly busy for a while there, but now I've got everything under control."

Michaela looked reassured, but Kaitlin felt uneasy. This business of having a relationship was even trickier than she'd thought.

All during English class, she found herself twisting her neck to glance at Connor. Once or twice he looked up at the same time and locked eyes with her. Embarrassed, she turned back around.

Anyone would think you were a middle-school girl with a bad case of puppy love instead of a senior in high school, she thought as her cheeks burned. *Well, no wonder. I'm way behind everyone else. I've spent the last few years learning about horses while other girls were learning about guys and dating.*

She had a lot to catch up on, that was for sure. She needed to study up quickly and figure out how to let Connor know she really did want to spend time with him.

It was just before the bell rang, dismissing English class, that her worries about Connor were cut off by thoughts of Sterling. She found herself wondering if Sam had remembered to turn her out in the paddock in the morning. Sam *had* looked awfully tired after the trial on Sunday. She was pregnant, after all, and carrying twins, no less! Maybe she'd slept in again and hadn't gotten around to the turnouts that day.

Don't be ridiculous, Kaitlin told herself. *Tor would do it. Or maybe Allie would. Sam always makes sure the horses are taken care of.*

But she couldn't stop worrying. The second the bell rang, Kaitlin sprang from her seat and ran into the hallway.

I'll just make a quick phone call to be sure. It was against the rules to use cell phones at school. Looking around furtively to make sure no teachers were coming, she held up her books while she punched in Whisperwood's number and hunched over her phone.

"You ran off awfully quickly," Connor said teasingly, coming up behind her and playfully poking her in the rib.

Kaitlin nearly jumped out of her skin. Frowning, she held up a finger and whispered, "Just a sec," as Sam answered.

"Sorry, I didn't see that you were on the phone," Connor apologized.

"Hey, Sam," Kaitlin said, speaking in a low voice. "It's me, Kaitlin. I wanted to know how Sterling was. Is she all right?"

"She's great," Sam replied. "I turned her out right after morning feeds. Why? Did you see something when you checked her this morning?"

"Uh, no," Kaitlin exclaimed as she squirmed uncomfortably. "I was just wondering if she got her turnout, that's all."

"She sure did. Everything's fine here," Sam said. "Don't you worry. I'll see you tomorrow after school."

"Okay," Kaitlin replied weakly. She paused before hanging up.

Slipping her phone back into her backpack, she turned back to Connor. "Sorry," she said.

Connor gave her a knowing look. "Don't tell me. Horses again, right?"

Kaitlin ran her fingers through her hair and nodded. "But it's all taken care of now."

"Good. Because I wanted to ask you to come with me and some friends for pizza after school tomorrow," Connor said just as the next bell rang. "You're not going to blow me off again because of horses, are you? I'm starting to feel kind of hurt here, being dumped for a bunch of whiskery equine types."

"You're not being dumped," Kaitlin said in a rush. "I'd love to come with you and your friends."

You've got a lesson tomorrow, Kaitlin reminded herself as she hugged her books to her chest and scurried to her next class.

Well, she decided, she'd just have to cancel. She'd come up with an excuse and call Sam right before evening feeds. There was no way she was going to ruin her chances with Connor now that things were starting to look so promising!

"Hey, Kaitlin—need a lift to Whisperwood, or did you drive that wreck on wheels of yours?" called Parker as he backed his truck out of a space in the senior parking lot the next day.

Kaitlin, who'd been walking by herself toward Connor's car, looked up, startled. Blinking, she shielded her eyes from the glare of the afternoon sun. "Parker? What are you doing here at good old Henry Clay?" she squeaked.

Parker grinned and stuck his head out his window. "Don't look so worried. They didn't kick me out of college and send me back to high school," he joked. "I was just stopping by to drop off my grandfather's pledge for the school library building fund."

Kaitlin swallowed. Seeing Parker reminded her that she hadn't called Sam to cancel her lesson. She'd put it totally out of her mind the day before when she'd decided at the last minute to go shopping for something to wear for the pizzeria get-together. Now she cast a quick glance at Connor's sports car, where she could see that he and his friends were waiting for her. One of the guys motioned for her to hurry.

"Oh," Kaitlin said lamely, trying to think fast.

"Pretty fancy duds you're wearing, by the way," Parker commented. "I take it you're not planning to slap your schooling chaps over them and wear them during your lesson."

"Ha ha, no," Kaitlin replied nervously. "I'm, um, not going to the barn this afternoon," she added, not daring to meet Parker's smoky gray eyes.

Parker raised an eyebrow. "But it's Tuesday. Aren't you riding with Sam in your usual four-thirty?"

Kaitlin shook her head. "I was supposed to," she replied. "But I'm not . . . feeling well."

Parker looked concerned. "That stomach flu bug got you after all, huh?"

"Yeah, that's right," Kaitlin said quickly. "It's just a touch. No biggie."

"Well, I guess Allie could ride Sterling for you. Feel better," Parker said, driving off.

Kaitlin scowled and watched his truck drive away before she continued walking toward Connor's car. On the way to the pizzeria, she used her cell phone to call Whisperwood. Luckily, she got the answering machine. It was much easier to wiggle out of her lesson by machine than to have to lie straight out to Sam.

A half hour later, she was squeezed into a crowded booth at the pizzeria, Connor on one side and Michaela on the other. She and Connor were sharing a humongous cheesy concoction. For a while she forgot all about Whisperwood as she joined in the playful banter around the table. But when the conversation turned to the school play, Kaitlin fell into silence and found her thoughts drifting back to the barn. Soon she felt the pizza forming a lump in her stomach. It was hard to enjoy herself when she felt guilty that she'd lied to get out of her lesson.

Oh, don't make such a big deal out of things, Boyce. It's just this one time, she told herself, leaning against Connor's shoulder for reassurance.

But when they were driving home and Connor asked if she wanted to go watch his rehearsal the next afternoon, Kaitlin shifted nervously in her seat. She didn't dare weasel out of her lessons two days in a row.

"I really—" she started to say, pausing to find the words to turn Connor down without making him feel dumped by horses again. But she couldn't think of a way. Finally she blurted out, "That'll be fun. I'd love to see you act."

Sam will never understand, she thought unhappily, turning toward the window.

The next day Kaitlin called the barn office during her lunch hour. She'd stayed up late the night before making a plan. She'd call at noon, when she knew Sam would be up at the house. That way the answering machine would pick up.

When she got home from the rehearsal, her mom looked at her. "Sam called here and left a message telling you she hoped you were getting better," she said. "I didn't know you weren't well. You should have stayed home from school if you were sick."

Kaitlin felt her face go pale. "Oh, it's nothing," she mumbled. "Just felt a little off, that's all."

She escaped to her room, hoping that her mom wouldn't come in and fuss over her because she thought Kaitlin was sick. She wasn't used to lying, and it made her feel terrible. Still, it was worth it. Connor had asked her to go with him to Soda Jerks, a fifties-style ice cream parlor, the next afternoon. There was no way she was missing that. After all, things were finally going smoothly with him, now that there weren't horses in the way.

After school on Thursday, Kaitlin rode with Connor to Soda Jerks. They found a booth with several kids from the theater club and ordered enormous mountains of ice cream and toppings. But as soon as the theater talk started up, she sipped at her soda and twisted a lock of her hair while gazing off into space. Looking around the space, she saw that, like many restaurants in Lexington, Soda Jerks boasted a bulletin board plastered with horse photos. Someone— maybe the soda fountain owner—must be a racing fan, Kaitlin decided.

The theater talk showed no signs of letting up, so after a while Kaitlin got up from the booth. She wandered over for a closer look at the bulletin board, where she saw photos and clippings of the usual racehorses as well as other horses. Seconds later her eye was caught by a photo of the same small horse pictured on the poster that used to be on her wall. In this photo, he was jumping a huge round-top fence, his knees snapping up perfectly.

He's so small, and yet look how huge he jumps. Who is this horse? she thought, tracing her finger over the horse's strong, muscular lines. *He must be famous.*

"I see you're a Charisma fan, too," said a small, black-haired waitress who stopped behind her. She was balancing a tray loaded with sundaes.

"Charisma?" Kaitlin repeated, glancing at her. If she remembered correctly, Charisma was the name of the race-horse Christina had been riding in the Belmont Fall Meet when she'd gotten hurt. But it was possible that there was another horse by that name.

The waitress nodded. "Amazing eventer. Won all kinds of Olympic medals back in the eighties with Mark Todd, and he was just named Horse of the Century by *Practical Horseman* magazine." She looked at Kaitlin, then stopped. "Sorry," she added with a nervous giggle. "I get carried away. I'm from New Zealand. You probably have no idea what I'm talking about. Most people in the States don't even know what eventing is."

"Actually, I do," Kaitlin started to say. But by then the waitress had walked off toward a table in the far corner.

Kaitlin studied the photo for a few more seconds before returning to her seat. "Charisma," she repeated to herself. "Mark Todd." Of course she'd heard of Mark Todd. He was a well-known eventer from New Zealand. But she'd never put it together that it was him on her poster. For months, she'd admired his form and wished she could ride like him.

She'd wondered just who the scopey horse was that was negotiating such a huge jump. Now she knew. Suddenly she was fired with curiosity and wanted to know more about the little horse who was such a standout that he'd been named Horse of the Century.

Lost in her thoughts, Kaitlin returned to the table. She hardly felt Connor's arm as he put it around her. Absently she raised a spoonful of rich, melting ice cream topped with nuts.

Just as she was about to take a huge bite, she looked up in time to see Sam walk through the front door. Allie followed her in, flanked by several Whisperwood students, including Justin, Penny, Morgan, and Lisa.

You are dead, Boyce, absolutely dead, Kaitlin thought, dropping her spoon and shrugging off Connor's arm.

She tried to sink low in the booth, but Lisa and Penny immediately spotted her.

"Look, look, it's Kaitlin! Hooray, she's all better!" Penny called out loudly above the din of the noisy restaurant, and headed over toward where Kaitlin was sitting.

Kaitlin froze as she saw Allie nudge Sam.

When she got to Kaitlin's table, Penny did a little pirouette, causing Connor's friends to stop talking and stare. "We've missed you. When are you coming back to ride?" Without waiting for an answer, she charged on, her face glowing with excitement. "Guess what? Sam said we all did so well last week at Deep Woods, she's treating us all to a Monster Mountain!"

"Great," Kaitlin said, knowing that Sam would certainly come over and let her have it for lying. *Here it comes*, she thought, her heart sinking when she saw Sam striding across the room.

Even from a distance, Kaitlin could see the fiery glint in her instructor's green eyes. Sam's freckles stood out against the angry flush of her cheeks. "Wow. I guess it must be a *very* exotic strain of stomach flu, huh?" she commented as she neared the table. She stared pointedly at the huge pile of ice cream sitting in front of Kaitlin. "Oh, never mind. C'mon, Penny."

Kaitlin's throat tightened as she watched the instructor and her students walk over to the counter.

"What was that all about?" Connor asked.

"Nothing," Kaitlin mumbled.

"That was another one of your riding instructors, right?" he asked.

Kaitlin nodded. *Was* was definitely the word, she thought miserably.

"Those horse people are always on your case," Connor observed. "What's up with that?"

"It's not that simple," Kaitlin murmured, her face flaming.

Connor touched her bruised cheek lightly with his fin-

138

gertips, then slowly turned back toward the other kids at the table.

Kaitlin sat there, toying idly with her spoon and eyeing the pile of ice cream as if it were poison. She wished she dared to jump up and run out of Soda Jerks. Instead, she sat rooted to her seat, overcome with guilt and humiliation.

Once or twice she stole a glance over at the Whisperwood group. The kids were wolfing down their treats, talking and laughing uproariously. At one point, Justin got up and galloped around the table, sending the kids into fits of giggles and causing Sam to shake her head wryly.

The little kids' innocent laughter seemed to cut right through Kaitlin. It reminded her of a time when riding well at an event had been huge and when horses had been the only thing that mattered.

When had everything changed and gotten to be so confusing?

When I grew up and stopped acting like a little horse-crazy kid, Kaitlin told herself fiercely. But somehow that realization didn't make her feel better.

When she and Connor got up to leave, Kaitlin was tempted to walk past the Whisperwood group without a word. But after a moment she made her way over to the table.

"See you tomorrow," she said quietly, looking directly at Sam.

Sam merely shrugged and turned to sip her soda.

Kaitlin stood there for a few seconds, knowing she should apologize for lying. But the words wouldn't come out.

Finally she said good-bye to the kids and walked to the door.

"Don't let it get to you. You don't need all that nonsense anyway," Connor said, protectively putting his arm around Kaitlin's waist as they approached the door.

Kaitlin bit her lip and didn't say anything.

SATURDAY MORNING KAITLIN SAT ON STERLING'S BACK IN THE
rear arena. Earlier she'd slipped in the barn the back way
and groomed the mare in her stall, hoping she wouldn't
run into anyone. It was probably all over Whisperwood
that she'd lied and faked being sick, and she couldn't bear
to face anyone. It would be hard enough facing Sam.

Luckily, though, Whisperwood was bustling with
activity, and Kaitlin had managed to saddle up and make
her way to the arena without crossing paths with any other
students.

As she adjusted her girth by the entrance, a cool wind
cut through her fleece. It blew up some leaves, causing
Sterling to snort and skitter. Kaitlin soothed her before

starting her warm-up walk. When she saw Sam coming toward the ring, she slowed Sterling at the rail by the gate, unsure what she would say. Nervously, she put both reins in one hand, then pulled at the fingers of her right glove with her teeth. Sterling danced as another gust of wind flipped up her tail, and Kaitlin hurriedly put both hands back on the reins to bring her under control.

"Sterling's feeling good this morning, I see," Sam said conversationally as she opened the gate and stepped into the arena.

"She sure is," Kaitlin said awkwardly, urging Sterling forward again.

Sam made her way to the center of the arena and folded her arms across her chest. "Allie did some light work on her the last few days," Sam commented as Kaitlin and Sterling picked up a working trot. "That girl does have a way with horses, I must say."

Kaitlin swallowed but didn't reply. She wondered when Sam would bring up her lie. As she rode around the arena she kept glancing at her instructor, waiting for her to say something. But Sam merely watched silently, her arms still crossed.

Finally Kaitlin couldn't stand it any longer. She trotted over to where Sam was sitting, and halted Sterling squarely in front of her.

"I'm—I'm sorry!" she exclaimed. "About everything."

Sam regarded her. "It's not me you need to apologize to, you know," she said quietly.

Kaitlin was puzzled. *Surely she doesn't expect me to apologize to Allie for having to ride Sterling for me*, she thought angrily.

"Do you know who I mean?" Sam asked.

Kaitlin shook her head.

"Sterling," Sam replied. "She's the one you've been letting down."

Kaitlin hung her head. For a few seconds she sat there, slumped in her saddle. She knew she deserved Sam's remarks, but it didn't make it any easier to take.

"You know, we never discussed Deep Woods," Sam said.

Kaitlin's head snapped up. "What is there to discuss?" she asked defensively. "I mean, we got around and all. Well, okay, except for the stadium jumping."

Sam raised an eyebrow.

Kaitlin went on. "Considering the way I've been riding, I thought I did all right," she flashed.

"You thought you did all right?" Sam echoed, shaking her head. "I never thought I'd hear you be satisfied with 'all right.' You were the girl who wanted to ride in the Olympics one day."

Kaitlin furrowed her brow. Funny how she hadn't thought about the Olympics much at all in the last few days. "Maybe I just have other things on my mind right now," she replied.

"Such as?" Sam tilted her head.

Thinking of Connor, Kaitlin smiled involuntarily. But she didn't answer Sam's question.

"A guy, perhaps?" When Kaitlin didn't respond, the instructor nodded. "You know, Kaitlin, it's okay to make room for others in your life," she said gently. "But like everything else connected with riding, it still comes down to balance."

"Try telling that to Connor," Kaitlin was surprised to hear herself say.

Sam pursed her lips. "So he doesn't understand how much time you need to spend with Sterling. Is that it?"

"Well, sort of," Kaitlin began, shifting in her saddle. "He was wondering why I couldn't ever go out with him. I could tell that he was ready to just give up and go find someone else. I didn't want that."

"No, I can see that," Sam commented with a thoughtful expression on her face.

Kaitlin suddenly went on the offensive. "The thing is," she burst out, "you and Parker never let up. One minute you're pushing me; the next you're telling me to relax and have fun. Can I help it if I'm totally confused?"

"Wait a minute. That's not fair," Sam replied, holding up her hand. "It takes work and consistency to compete at the preliminary level. If you don't put in the time, you or Sterling could end up getting seriously hurt. If Parker or I have done anything, it's that we tried to keep both of you safe. But that doesn't mean that sometimes we both see that you need to back off a little at times if you're going to meet your goals."

Kaitlin digested this for a few seconds. Then she said quietly, "Maybe it's just that. Maybe my goals have changed."

Sam suddenly locked eyes with her. "Maybe they have," she said. "And that's okay. But the thing is, Sterling hasn't changed. She still needs love and attention. She still wants to do her job. But she can't do it when your heart and mind are elsewhere. It's a partnership, remember?"

"What are you getting at?" Kaitlin asked sharply.

"Maybe we need to reconsider our leasing arrangement with Sterling," Sam said.

Kaitlin couldn't believe her ears. Sam was terminating Sterling's lease?

"Fine!" she shot back, reining Sterling sharply and trotting out of the arena. If that was the way Sam wanted it, then she could have Sterling back!

She rode hotly toward the barn, overtaking Parker, who was leading Black Hawke.

"Slow down or I'll have to ticket you," he called.

"You'll be glad to hear that I've just quit riding, and I'm

turning Sterling back over to Sam," she retorted.

"What?" Parker yelped. "What gives?"

Kaitlin stopped and jumped off, turning to face Parker. "I quit, that's all," she said.

Parker's jaw tightened. "You can't quit," he said.

"Watch me," Kaitlin replied.

Parker stared at her dumbly, not speaking for a moment. "I've got a quote for you, then, since apparently you're so big on them lately," he murmured. Taking a deep breath, he said softly, "'Riding a horse is not a gentle hobby to be picked up and laid down like a game of solitaire. It is a grand passion.'"

"Maybe for some people," Kaitlin shot back, walking past him.

Kaitlin had just loosened Sterling's girth and run up the stirrup irons when tears started welling up in her eyes. She wiped them away just as Christina appeared in the doorway.

"Omigosh, Kaitlin. What's wrong?" Christina asked, maneuvering her crutches toward her.

Kaitlin gulped and wiped her eyes. "Nothing. I'm fine," she lied.

Christina shook her head. "No, you're not," she replied. She stood there quietly, waiting for Kaitlin to speak.

Kaitlin pulled Sterling's reins over her head. "You're right, I'm not," she admitted. "I guess you might as well know—Sam's asked me to give up the lease on Sterling."

Christina's face registered complete shock. Her face went pale, and her jaw dropped. "What?" she gasped.

Kaitlin heard herself talking quickly in a voice she hardly recognized. "I've—I've moved on, that's all," she said. "I don't have time for horses anymore."

"What *are* you talking about?" Christina asked. "Moved on?"

Kaitlin tossed her head. "That's right," she replied. "Excuse me, I've got some work to do."

Christina stood her ground. "So you're just going to walk away and forget all about Sterling, just like that, huh?" she said. "Wow. I guess I was way wrong about you."

"What's that supposed to mean?" Kaitlin challenged her.

Christina stood aside. "Nothing," she muttered. "Forget it." She placed her crutches under her arms and clomped down the aisle. Then she turned around and clomped back.

"You know, it nearly killed me to give up Sterling and all my eventing dreams for her," she said, her eyes flashing. "But I had to if I was going to give Star his chance at the Triple Crown, so I sold her to Sam. I didn't want to, but I knew it would be all right, because I knew you were going to ride Sterling and that you were going to give her her shot at greatness. And now look! You're going to toss her out of your life like—like an old dishrag!"

Kaitlin felt as though she'd just received a body blow. "I'm not tossing her out!" she practically shouted. "And anyway, Sam can just find someone else who can event her."

Christina pursed her lips and retorted, "Go ahead and think that if it makes you feel better." Stalking off, she turned to call over her shoulder, "I'm going to talk to Allie."

Kaitlin winced. Not wanting to explode, she gave Sterling's lead a little tug and walked away quickly. When she'd finished with Sterling, she closed her stall one last time.

"Be good, okay, girl?" she said, tears blurring her vision as she reached through the bars to touch the mare's soft muzzle.

Trying not to think about what she was doing, Kaitlin picked up her tack and grooming box and carried it to her car, dumping it in a heap in the backseat. She drove out of the driveway without saying good-bye to anyone—and without looking back.

On Monday during lunch, Kaitlin ducked into the school library to check out some books she needed for her Emerson paper that was due at midweek. Instead of working on her paper, she'd spent most of the weekend moping around the house and trying not to replay the wrenching whinny Sterling had let out when she'd left the barn. She'd hoped Connor would call to distract her, but she didn't hear from him till late Sunday. When she hung up after talking with him, she'd been surprised at how hollow she still felt.

It'll be better when I see him during English this afternoon, she thought while she combed the shelves looking for the titles she needed.

She had just reached for a book on the top shelf when suddenly she heard Connor's voice. It sounded like he was in the next row. She was just about to walk around the shelf to go greet him when she heard a giggle that made her pause.

"Well, well, well, if it isn't Connor Hamilton. I didn't expect to find you in the library." Kaitlin recognized the voice immediately—it was Madison. She knew she shouldn't eavesdrop, but still she stayed, straining to hear Connor's reply.

"What are you saying? That I don't ever read?" Connor pretended to sound hurt.

"No, but you have to admit you usually don't hang out here during lunch hour," Madison exclaimed. "Normally the only ones here are the hopeless study geeks, like Stephanie Heyerdorff over there."

Connor laughed. "Ouch. Don't compare me to Stephanie," he said in a low voice. "She practically lives here. Definitely a girl who could stand to get a life."

Get a life. That phrase again. Kaitlin flashed back to the other night when Connor had said that to her. She bit her lip as her gaze drifted over to where Stephanie sat, hunched over her books. She'd always admired the hardworking girl. Once Stephanie had confessed to her that her dream was to be a cardiologist and fly around treating people in impoverished countries. It was a life, all right—a good one. So what if it meant that Stephanie had to give up some other things to make it happen?

Suddenly Kaitlin was struck by the similarity between her goal and Stephanie's. They both required people to dedicate themselves to the dream if they wanted to achieve it.

People like Madison will never understand that kind of commitment, Kaitlin thought. Then she sucked in her breath as she realized that Connor had more or less gone along with Madison's assessment.

Suddenly her Emerson books fell with a clatter. As she bent over, she saw that one of the books had opened. The quotation that Parker had rattled off to her now danced off the page: *Riding a horse is not a gentle hobby to be picked up and laid down like a game of solitaire. It is a grand passion.*

"So it was Emerson who wrote it," Kaitlin said aloud. Clutching her books, she suddenly made a beeline for the checkout desk and didn't stop when Connor called out her name.

During English class, Kaitlin ignored the note that Connor flipped on her desk. When the dismissal bell rang, she shot up from her seat and darted out in the hallway, moving quickly in case he tried to follow.

Her brain was full of images of Sterling jumping formidable fences the way Charisma did—and there was no room to worry about Connor and his version of how she should live her life.

After school, she immediately made her way to the senior parking lot, where she jumped into her car. It seemed to drive itself straight to Whisperwood.

Once she'd stopped in the parking area by the stable, Kaitlin felt her nerve drain from her. It was one thing to make up her mind that she'd made a huge mistake by giving up Sterling. It was another to waltz back into Sam's office and try to convince her that she'd give anything to have her beloved mare back.

How can I make her see that I'm really serious? Kaitlin thought, fighting back tears. She sat in the car for a few minutes, gazing around at Whisperwood's spacious grounds. Suddenly she caught sight of Sterling in a nearby field. The mare had just lifted her head to drink in the wind. The sun was behind her, so she was backlit, her dappled gray coat shimmering. *Without a doubt,* Kaitlin thought, *Sterling is the most beautiful horse to ever set hooves in a paddock. What if I've lost her forever?*

Kaitlin put her face in her hands and gave way to racking sobs.

A sudden tapping on her window made her look up. It was Parker.

Kaitlin opened her window a tiny bit. "Oh, go away," she sobbed.

Parker crossed his arms in front of his chest. "Nuh-uh," he said.

"I mean it," Kaitlin snuffled loudly.

Parker shook his head. "So do I," he tossed back. "I'm not moving till you tell me why you're in flash-flood mode."

Kaitlin smiled weakly in spite of her tears. Trust Parker to make a joke just when she was more devastated than she ever had been in her whole life. Reluctantly she opened her car door and climbed out.

"You're the biggest pain, you know that?" she said, wiping her eyes.

Parker uncrossed his arms and grinned. "Yup. But that still doesn't let you off the hook. Spill it. And I don't mean tears."

"Fine," Kaitlin said, realizing just how eager she was to talk to someone who maybe could understand. After all, Parker dreamed of the Olympics, and he too had to endure his share of problems along the way.

"I guess you're furious about Sterling," she said, looking down at the dirt by Parker's paddock boots.

"Yeah, but I still don't believe it," Parker replied.

"Well, it's true. I told Sam it was fine if she wanted to terminate the lease. I thought I'd feel better once I made up my mind to let Sterling go, but I don't. I feel horrible." Kaitlin suddenly felt her throat tighten.

Parker fixed her with a penetrating stare. "I still can't believe you'd give up riding," he said. "Is this about Mr. Dressage Is Boring?"

Kaitlin made no reply.

"You're having trouble figuring out how to fit him in and fit in your plans for Sterling."

Kaitlin's head snapped up. "Oh, I guess you know," she said.

"Well, duh. I'm not totally blind, even if I *am* a guy," Parker said, tossing back the jibe that Kaitlin had thrown to him earlier in the month.

"I shouldn't have said that," Kaitlin confessed.

"Whatever," Parker said. "Keep talking."

"The thing is, I thought that the problem was trying to fit them both into my life. So I decided horses—Sterling— had to go. But I was wrong. I'm so miserable thinking about losing her that I just can't stand it." Kaitlin paused and gulped before going on. "I want to go beg Sam to let me have her back. And if I'm lucky enough to get to lease her again, that still puts me right back where I started."

"How so?" Parker asked. "So you just tell this Connor guy that this is how it is if he wants to hang with you. It's pretty simple."

Kaitlin snorted. "Oh, that's rich. I know you didn't say any such thing to Christina," she sputtered, almost laughing in spite of her misery. "She's not the kind of girl to take that one meekly."

Now Parker's cheeks flamed. "You're right about that," he admitted. "We did have to talk it out a few times, and we did have to agree to stand back and let each other go after what we wanted. But I'm telling you that it can be done."

"With the right person," Kaitlin said, in a voice barely above a whisper. "How do you know if the person you like is the right person?"

Parker held up his hands. "I can't help you there," he said. "You're the only one who can figure that out. But all I can say is, dealing with relationships is kind of like working with horses. You can't force things. You can't muscle them and try to get them to bend to your will. Sometimes you have to stand back and look for a little balance."

"Oh, Parker, honestly!" Kaitlin said, shaking her head and trying not to laugh. "You're sweet to try to help, but maybe you ought to stick to teaching me about eventing."

"I think you're right," Parker said, wiping his brow. "I'm definitely not the love advisor. Now my next piece of advice is, if you want to be an eventer, you'd better make sure you've got a good horse to ride. So if I were you, I'd hightail it into Sam's office and grovel for Sterling like you've never groveled before."

Kaitlin suddenly felt her heart lift. Impulsively she hugged Parker for all she was worth.

When she released him, she took a deep breath. Then she walked purposefully toward Sam, who had just appeared around the corner and nearly dropped her riding schedules when she saw Kaitlin. And Kaitlin, for her part, told Sam *everything* she needed to hear.

Hours later, Kaitlin dimmed the lights in the living room and clicked the DVD remote. Soon the images from *Eventing Greats* played across the screen. She watched scene after scene of great horse-and-rider teams. Burghley. Badminton. Gatcombe. The images raced past her, barely registering in her consciousness.

But when she came to one grainy part featuring the 1984 Olympics, she sat up as she saw a familiar little horse gallop his way to greatness over the cross-country course.

"Unbelievable," she murmured as she watched him whip joyfully across the finish line.

Afterward she replaced her horse things around her room. The last thing she put back was her poster of the legendary Charisma and Mark Todd. Though it was wrinkled, it still showcased Charisma's fiery spirit.

"Someday Sterling and I are going to win a gold, just like you did," she vowed, touching Charisma's shoulder with her fingertips. "Nothing's going to stop us."

13

"WELL DONE," SAM SAID AFTER KAITLIN HAD FINISHED AN intense dressage session several days later. "I hardly saw you lean at all."

Kaitlin took off her helmet and grinned like an idiot. "That's because I've been doing my leg-strengthening exercises," she said.

"I don't think your remarkable turnaround was entirely due to leg exercises," Sam said dubiously.

"Maybe not entirely," Kaitlin conceded. "But I just made up my mind that I was going to enjoy riding again. I'm working on my leg exercises, but I'm not letting my riding worries take over completely anymore."

Sam nodded. "Balance," she said simply. "Horsemanship is a mind, body, and spirit thing, you know. I think it's finally starting to click. And that's a start."

Kaitlin reached down to pat Sterling. For a long time after Sam walked back to the barn, Kaitlin lingered and rode Sterling slowly around for her cooldown, a smile still on her face. She had just dismounted and was headed toward the gate when she saw Connor striding toward them.

Oh, great, she thought, her heart plummeting to her boots. *I just get my head back on straight, and now he has to come here and throw me off again.*

She studied Connor making his way toward her, the feeling in her stomach worse than any kick from a horse could ever be. She hadn't expected it to hurt so much to break it off with him, especially since it had never quite gotten off the ground in the first place.

Taking a deep breath, Kaitlin touched Sterling's sides with her heels and rode up to meet him by the gate. She wished she didn't feel like jumping down and throwing her arms around his neck.

"Hi," Connor said as she drew up in front of him.

"Hi," Kaitlin responded, trying to look cool and perfectly in control.

"You're probably wondering what I'm doing here," he said, a muscle in his jaw twitching.

"Well, yeah," Kaitlin replied. "That kind of sums it up."

The last time she'd spoken to him had been two days earlier, when she'd told him that she was sorry but that she couldn't see him anymore.

"You see, I've thought about it, and I've decided there's no way I'm giving up my horses," she had said, talking in a rush. "It would be like me asking you to give up theater. I wouldn't dream of doing that. I'll bet it would kill you to have to throw away something that means so much to you." Then she'd walked away, not at all surprised that he hadn't followed.

Now she sat waiting while Sterling jingled her bit impatiently. He was probably going to unload on her, Kaitlin decided, and tell her that she had no life or something. But that was fine—his words didn't have any power over her anymore.

But Connor didn't unload. Instead he reached for her gloved hand. "I've missed you," he said simply. "And I've realized what a jerk I've been, pressing you to push aside your horses so we could be together all the time."

Kaitlin's jaw dropped, and she tried to pull her hand away. Connor, however, wouldn't let go, and he plowed on. "I tried to impress you, making you think I knew more about horses than I did, just to win you over," he confessed. "I got those horse quotes from the Shakespeare play I'm in, and I let on that I've ridden more than I actually have. The real deal is that I was in a TV commercial once, back in

Florida. I had to ride a horse while I was eating this yogurt-on-the-go stuff. So I took a couple of lessons. But other than that, I haven't really been around horses that much. I was being an actor—in more ways than one, I guess."

So that explains it, Kaitlin thought, remembering how uneasy he'd been around Sterling and how he hadn't understood when they'd had to hold back from galloping Megaton.

"Why would you go through all that trouble of faking the horse thing just for me?" Kaitlin asked.

Without waiting for an answer, she clucked at Sterling and cued her to walk out the gate. She knew Sterling could tell that her mind was elsewhere. When the mare reached a patch of grass, she reached down to snatch a mouthful before Kaitlin picked up her head again.

"Do I have to spell it out?" Connor asked. "It's because I really like you."

Kaitlin swallowed. "You probably shouldn't," she said. "It'll never work out. I'm not like the girls you're used to. I'm shy. I say stupid things. I'm usually covered with horse-hair. I have a million things to do, and I just can't drop them when it's inconvenient."

"Never mind all that. It's not important," Connor said, his eyes boring into hers. "I just know that I was wrong and that I want to be with you, even if I have to share you with the horses. I came here to see if maybe we could start over and get things right this time."

160

Kaitlin studied his face for a few moments, not sure whether to believe him. But then it occurred to her that he had no reason to come here to talk to her if he didn't mean it.

"I don't know," she said slowly. "Things haven't changed. I need to spend my time out here, with Sterling. I want to go to the Olympics one day, and in the meantime I've got a lot of work to do. I don't always have time to go out, even if I want to."

Connor nodded. "I know that," he said. "That's why I just went and signed up for some lessons with some girl named Christina in the barn office. That way I can still see you even when you're busy out here with Sterling."

"You did that for me?" Kaitlin asked in disbelief.

"Well, for me, too," Connor admitted. "I know I told you dressage was boring, but I have always wanted to jump. That seems kind of cool. And I figured that career-wise, it wouldn't hurt to be able to ride, really ride. Casting directors are always looking for actors who can ride for one role or another."

"There's more to horses than riding, you know," Kaitlin said, trying to process all this.

"I kind of figured that out from watching you and Sterling," Connor said. "But I want to learn. So how about it?"

Kaitlin looked up and scanned the trees surrounding Whisperwood, playing for time while she decided how to respond. Finally she nodded. "I'm willing to give it a try if you are," she said.

161

Connor grinned and patted Sterling, who promptly snorted, showering his white shirt with gobs of partially chewed green grass.

"I guess this is the way it's going to be," he said, his eyes dancing as he surveyed the mess.

Kaitlin burst out laughing. "Guess so," she said happily, turning Sterling toward the barn.

Charisma with his rider, Mark Todd.

Charisma

October 30, 1972–January 7, 2003

Charisma, known affectionately as "Podge," was a small horse (15.3 hands) who left a big impression on the eventing world.

This New Zealand–bred gelding was part Thoroughbred and part Percheron. He loved to eat, which was how he earned his nickname. Charisma was noted for his intelligence and personality. Though he was considered undersized by eventing standards, he was a good mover with a big stride. This made him seem larger than he was. Possessing a scopey jump and a bold, forward style, Charisma took his rider, Mark Todd, to individual Olympic gold medals at Los Angeles in 1984 and Seoul in 1988. He was only the second horse in Olympic history to win in two consecutive Olympics.

In addition to his Olympic gold, Charisma took second place twice at Badminton and a second at Burghley in 1987. He also won two British Open Eventing Championships.

Once Charisma retired, he went home to New Zealand, where he lived the life of a celebrity for many years. In 2003, he was put down humanely at the age of thirty, after being found with a broken shoulder in his paddock at Rivermonte Farm.

Karle Dickerson grew up riding, reading, and dreaming about horses. This is the eighth horse book she has written. She has shown in hunters and dressage, worked at a Thoroughbred breeding farm, and has been on cattle drives in Wyoming. She and her family used to own a horse ranch, and have always had numerous horses and ponies. The latest include two Thoroughbreds off the track named Cezanne and Earl Gray, and a gray Welsh pony named Magpie.

WIN
A BREYER COLLECTIBLE PORCELAIN HORSE!

ENTER THE
THOROUGHBRED BREYER COLLECTIBLE PORCELAIN HORSE
SWEEPSTAKES!

COMPLETE THIS ENTRY FORM • NO PURCHASE NECESSARY

NAME: _____

ADDRESS: _____

CITY: _____ STATE: _____ ZIP:_____

PHONE: _____ AGE: _____

MAIL TO: THOROUGHBRED BREYER COLLECTIBLE
PORCELAIN HORSE SWEEPSTAKES!
c/o HarperCollins, Attn.: Children's Marketing Department
10 E. 53rd Street New York, NY 10022

HarperEntertainment

17th Street Productions,
an Alloy Online, Inc., company

THOROUGHBRED 68 SWEEPSTAKES RULES
———————— OFFICIAL RULES ————————

1. No purchase necessary.

2. To enter, complete the official entry form or hand print your name, address, and phone number along with the words "Thoroughbred Breyer Collectible Porcelain Horse Sweepstakes" on a 3" x 5" card and mail to: HarperCollins, Attn.: Children's Marketing Department, 10 E. 53rd Street, New York, NY 10022. Entries must be received by February 28, 2005. Enter as often as you wish, but each entry must be mailed separately. One entry per envelope. Partially completed, illegible, or mechanically reproduced entries will not be accepted. Sponsors are not responsible for lost, late, mutilated, illegible, stolen, postage-due, incomplete, or misdirected entries. All entries become the property of HarperCollins and will not be returned.

3. The sweepstakes are open to all legal residents of the United States (excluding residents of Colorado and Rhode Island), who are between the ages of eight

and sixteen by February 28, 2005, excluding employees and immediate family members of HarperCollins, Alloy Online, Inc., or 17th Street Productions, an Alloy Online, Inc. company, and their respective subsidiaries, and affiliates, officers, directors, shareholders, employees, agents, attorneys, and other representatives (individually and collectively), and their respective parent companies, affiliates, subsidiaries, advertising, promotion and fulfillments agencies, and the persons with whom each of the above are domiciled. Offer void where prohibited or restricted.

4. Odds of winning depend on total number of entries received. Approximately 75,000 entry forms have been distributed. All prizes will be awarded. Winners will be randomly drawn on or about March 15, 2005 by representatives of HarperCollins, whose decisions are final. Potential winners will be notified by mail, and a parent or guardian of the potential winner will be required to sign and return an affadavit of eligibility and release of liability within 14 days of notification. Failure to return the affadavit within the time period will disqualify the winner and another winner will be chosen. By acceptance of the prize, the winner consents to the use of his or her name, photographs, likeness, and personal information by HarperCollins, Alloy Online, Inc., and 17th Street Productions, an Alloy Online, Inc. company, for publicity and advertising purposes without further compensation except where prohibited.

5. Ten (10) Grand Prize Winners will receive a Breyer collectible porcelain horse. HarperCollins reserves the right at its sole discretion to substitute another prize of equal or of greater value in the event this prize is unavailable. Approximate retail value totals $100.00.

6. Only one prize will be awarded per individual, family, or household. Prizes are nontransferable and cannot be sold or redeemed for cash. No cash substitute is available except at the sole discretion of HarperCollins for reasons of prize unavailability. Any federal, state, or local taxes are the responsibility of the winner.

7. Additional terms: By participating, entrants agree a) to the official rules and decisions of the judges, which will be final in all respects; and b) to release, discharge, and hold harmless HarperCollins, Alloy Online, Inc., and 17th Street Productions, an Alloy Online, Inc. company, and their affiliates, subsidiaries, and advertising promotion agencies from and against any and all liability or damages associated with acceptance, use, or misuse of any prize received in this sweepstakes.

8. To obtain the name of the winners, please send your request and a self-addressed stamped envelope (Vermont residents may omit return postage) to "Thoroughbred Free Porcelain Horse Winners List" c/o HarperCollins, Attn.: Children's Marketing Department, 10 E. 53rd Street, New York, NY 10022.

SPONSOR: HarperCollins Publishers Inc.